Joanne was forced to admit the truth

She was in love with her husband, Daniel Grant.

For the two years she'd worked with him she had fought against her love, labeling it admiration and respect. Now, her defenses rudely smashed, she experienced the pain and futility of her feelings for the man she had married.

Perhaps subconsciously she had always guarded herself against this truth. Now there was no longer anything to shield her from the agonizing realization that to Daniel she was nothing but the means of satisfying his mother's obsession to see him married before she died.

For hadn't Daniel said, "Rest assured I don't desire you, Joanne. You have nothing to fear...."

OTHER

Harlequin Romances

by YVONNE WHITTAL

Many of these titles are available at your local bookseller
or through the Harlequin Reader Service.

For a free catalogue listing all available Harlequin Romances,
send your name and address to:

HARLEQUIN READER SERVICE,
M.P.O. Box 707, Niagara Falls, N.Y. 14302
Canadian address: Stratford, Ontario, Canada N5A 6W2

or use coupon at back of book.

Love Is Eternal

by

YVONNE WHITTAL

Harlequin Books

TORONTO • LONDON • NEW YORK • AMSTERDAM
SYDNEY • HAMBURG • PARIS

Original hardcover edition published in 1978
by Mills & Boon Limited

ISBN 0-373-02249-2

Harlequin edition published April 1979

CHAPTER ONE

JOANNE WEBSTER faced her late Uncle Steven's lawyer across the wide expanse of his desk. She had called on Samuel Davidson with a purpose, yet at this point she hesitated, and her hesitation invoked a feeling of sympathy in the stern-looking man who sat drumming absently on his desk blotter with the tips of his blunt fingers, the hum of the air-conditioner the only other sound to disturb the uncomfortable silence.

'You came to see me about the last will and testament of your late uncle, Mr Steven Webster?' he prompted gently, and Joanne's long, dark lashes flew upwards to unveil clear green eyes that registered surprise and a certain amount of anxiety as they met the lawyer's.

'Mr Davidson, perhaps I should explain.' Her well-modulated voice possessed a quality of warmth that never failed to attract attention, and to soothe those listening to her. Mr Davidson was no exception, for his tired eyes registered surprised pleasure as he leaned back in his leather chair and prepared himself to listen. 'My brother and I were left more or less destitute when my parents died in a car accident five years ago. I had only just started my training as a nurse, and Bruce—my brother—still had to complete three years at school. Uncle Steven took pity on us and paid for Bruce's education. Then, knowing how desperately Bruce wanted to become an engineer like himself, Uncle Steven offered to pay whatever expenses Bruce would have in order to attend university. Bruce and I considered this a loan, and we accepted it on the understanding that we repaid it once Bruce has qualified. That was two years ago,' Joanne ended lamely, 'and my brother still has several years to go before he can start earning a living.'

'And now you want to know if your aunt will continue with the loan. Am I correct?'

Joanne nodded, nervously fingering the strap of her handbag. 'Nothing was written down to this effect, and I wondered if my uncle perhaps mentioned something about it in his will.'

Samuel Davidson's fingers resumed their drumming on the blotter, and Joanne began to feel like a watch that was being wound too tightly.

Samuel Davidson cleared his throat unnecessarily, and she experienced a sense of foreboding. 'If you had not made this appointment to call on me this afternoon, you would have received a letter shortly, instructing you to pay me a visit. I'm afraid, Miss Webster, that I have some unpleasant news for you.'

'Are you trying to tell me that the loan was never mentioned in my uncle's will?' Joanne asked, steeling herself against the inevitable.

'I'm afraid so, Miss Webster,' Samuel Davidson confirmed her suspicions. 'And your uncle's wife, Mrs Irene Webster, has instructed me to inform you that she has no intention of continuing with the loan.'

It was to be expected, Joanne thought unhappily. Irene, with no children of her own, had never made a secret of the fact that she disliked the idea of her husband giving financial help to his late brother's children, and her personal dislike of them had been just as evident.

'Do you realise what this means, Mr Davidson?' she

asked, controlling the tremor in her voice with difficulty. 'It means that my brother will have to discontinue his studies if I'm unable to find the money somewhere with which to help him. Oh, I've saved up a certain amount over the years with which I'd hoped to help him repay the loan one day, but the entire amount wouldn't be enough to keep him at university for another six months, let alone several years.'

Samuel Davidson's sympathetic glance rested momentarily on her pale cheeks before lingering on her pink, quivering lips. 'Perhaps if you discussed this with your aunt ...'

'No! Never!' she said adamantly. 'Bruce and I never asked Uncle Steven for any financial help. What he did for us, he did of his own free will, and we appreciated it tremendously, but I have no intention of going on my knees to Irene Webster. As far as *she's* concerned we're the poor relations who should never have trespassed beyond her kitchen door.'

Samuel Davidson looked taken aback. 'Is there no one else you could approach for a loan?'

Joanne swallowed with difficulty. 'We have no one else, Mr Davidson, and no bank would give me a loan without someone standing security.'

There was a strained silence in the room before Samuel Davidson spoke with deep sincerity. 'I understand what this must mean to you, Miss Webster, and if it were in my power to help you in some way, I would, but, as it is, there's nothing I can do. If Mr Webster had made a stipulation in his will concerning the loan, then nothing, and no one would have been able to alter the situation.'

Joanne rose to her feet, tall and slim in her pale green suit. 'It was kind of you to see me, Mr Davidson, and

I'm sorry to have taken up so much of your time.'

'It was my pleasure, Miss Webster,' he said instantly, taking the hand she extended towards him and holding it a moment longer than necessary.

After the cool interior of Mr Davidson's offices, Joanne welcomed the warm sunlight on her pale cheeks as she stepped out on to the pavement that January afternoon in Cape Town, and walked the short distance to the tea-room where Bruce eagerly awaited her return.

'What on earth am I going to tell him?' she wondered frantically as she waited at the pedestrian crossing for the lights to change. 'How do I tell him that his hopes for the future have become worthless dreams?'

The lights changed and Joanne crossed the street, oblivious of the appreciative glances turned in her direction while she wrestled with her problem. Her pace slowed when she reached the other side. The tea-room was just a block away, and she needed time to think. There had to be *some* way of getting the money they needed, but her prospects were nil, and she knew it. If only ...

Joanne pulled herself together. It was useless dwelling on something she did not have the power to change, she decided firmly.

Bruce, fair and slim, rose expectantly as she entered the tea-room, and Joanne's heart twisted with agony. He was all that she had, and she could not let him down.

'What's the verdict?' he asked when she joined him at the corner table, but her expression must have given him a clue. 'It wasn't good, was it?'

'I'm afraid it was worse than I expected.' Bruce faced her in silence and there was no way she could soften the blow. 'Uncle Steven made no provision in his will for the loan, and Aunt Irene has stated that she doesn't want to continue with it.'

Bruce looked crestfallen, but his determination matched Joanne's. 'Then there's only one thing I can do. I'll have to give up this temporary job I've taken for the holidays, find myself a permanent job, and study part-time.'

'No!' Joanne lowered her voice instantly as heads turned in their direction. 'I won't let you do that. Not yet, anyway.'

'Jo, there's nothing much else I can do,' he persisted doggedly. 'You don't have the money, do you?'

'I have something saved, but not enough,' she was forced to admit sadly.

'Then the matter is settled.'

'Bruce, you'll never make it that way,' she pleaded. 'Give me a little time, and I might just come up with something.'

His features broke into a reluctant smile. 'Knowing you, Jo, you'll move heaven and earth to help me, but don't do anything foolish. Not on my account, please!'

Joanne smiled for the first time, a warmth and a tenderness in her glance as it rested on the young man seated opposite her. 'We have a month before the university re-opens, and that should give us enough time to think of an alternative.'

Joanna might have sounded hopeful, but in her heart she knew the dreaded feeling of defeat. It would be so easy to let Bruce take a permanent job somewhere. He could still keep the flat he shared with a fellow student, but she knew he would soon discover how little time that would leave him for his studies, and, eventually, he would be forced to abandon his dream, to become as dissatisfied as their father had been. No, she *would* not allow it.

They parted company eventually, and Joanne took the bus to her small flat near the hospital where she worked as a theatre Sister. The journey took less than a half hour and, when she eventually turned the key in the lock of her door, a feeling of desolation swept over her. She pushed open the door and closed it behind her with a sigh, staring about her for a moment as if she were seeing the interior of her flat for the first time, from the drab curtains on the windows down to the worn carpet on the floor. She had saved her money so religiously over the past years that there had been little left for luxuries. Uncle Steven's loan had provided enough for Bruce, but she was determined to have enough saved to help him repay the loan one day. Now Uncle Steven was no longer there, the money he had loaned them to that date still had to be repaid, and an even larger amount had to be found for Bruce to continue his studies.

It was impossible, she realised, burying her face in her hands. No matter how much she thought about it, there seemed to be no way of acquiring the money she needed.

'Oh, what a mess!' she sighed, pushing herself away from the door and going through to her room.

She kicked off her shoes and took off her suit, hanging it neatly on a hanger in the wardrobe before she wrapped a thin housecoat about her and went through to the kitchen to make a strong pot of tea. Heaven only knew what she was going to do, she thought as she switched on the kettle, but she would have to find a solution—and find it soon.

A week later Joanne was no nearer to solving her problem, and it was beginning to have a serious effect on her work. Twice that morning she had passed Dr Grant the wrong instrument during a delicate operation to restore a man's features to normality. Dr Grant's blue eyes above his mask had at first been surprised, then downright angry when it happened a second time. She had murmured apologetically, forcing herself to concentrate, but the mistakes had been made, and Dr Grant would have every right to ask for a replacement.

Nothing happened, however, and Joanne's nerves settled as the day drew to a close. She had had a narrow escape, and she would have to watch her step in future.

When she finally went off duty shortly after six that evening she was weary to the extreme, and longed only for a hot, relaxing bath before seeking her bed, but, as she approached the bus stop, a large, powerful-looking car drew up beside her.

Joanne stepped back automatically, but the door on the passenger side was flung open, and Dr Grant's voice said authoritatively, 'Get in!'

Joanne reacted to the command in that voice as if he had snapped an order in the operating theatre and, seated beside him, the powerful car was set in motion once again.

'Dr Grant, I'm sorry about——'

'Later,' he snapped, and Joanne shrank meekly into her corner, dreading this private confrontation with this man who could be so formidable at times.

She should have known that Daniel Grant was not the kind of man who would run to Matron with complaints, and that he would deal with the matter in his own manner. She was not too sure at that moment which she would have preferred, Matron's sharp tongue, or Daniel Grant's wrath.

She stole a glance at him, but his expression gave her no indication of his thoughts. She admired his skill as a plastic surgeon and, after working with him in the theatre for almost two years, she had grown accustomed to his abruptness, and the almost menacing attitude he adopted when something was not to his liking.

Tall and lean, with raven-black hair and piercing blue eyes, he had most of the nursing staff practically swooning over him, but he appeared to be unaware of their adoration. He was attractive; *too* attractive, Joanne had thought on many occasions, and her admiration and respect had often bordered on something far deeper which she had had to clamp down severely. They had seldom spoken to each other out of the theatre, but here she was, seated beside him in his car, and being driven she knew not where.

It was ridiculous, she thought nervously. He could have reprimanded her in the privacy of her office without going to such lengths to see her alone.

The car slowed down and she glanced about her with interest for the first time. He had brought her to an out-of-the-way coffee bar and, after parking the car, he ushered her inside as if he was in a hurry to get this distasteful matter over and done with.

'Right, let's have it,' he said without preamble the moment their coffee was served. 'What's been eating you up inside this past week?'

It was not a question, but an order, and so very typical of the man. 'Why should there be something troubling me?'

'Look, Sister Webster ... Joanne.' He pinned her to her chair with his incredible blue eyes. 'May I call you Joanne?'

Startled, she could do no more than nod, her name sounding strange on his lips.

'There must be something wrong, Joanne, when a responsible and conscientious theatre Sister suddenly becomes scatterbrained,' he continued, his voice deep and gravelly. 'Either you tell me what it is so that we can sort it out and get things back to normal, or I shall be forced to ask for a replacement.'

'You're welcome to do that, Dr Grant,' she said, her chin raised proudly, but the faint quiver of her lips did not go undetected.

'Come now, Joanne,' he said impatiently. 'You know as well as I do that it would be difficult to replace you.'

A compliment from Dr Daniel Grant was something unheard of, and an odd sense of pleasure stole through her as she said: 'It's a private matter, Dr Grant.'

'No longer, it isn't,' he contradicted strongly. 'From the moment you brought it into the theatre it became my problem as well as yours. So out with it, Joanne Webster, and make it quick.'

Joanne stared at him for a moment, taking in the lean features, the dark, questioning brows, the straight, high-bridged nose and firm but perfectly chiselled mouth. Perhaps, she thought tiredly, it might just help to talk to someone about her problem, and sharing her load with Daniel Grant might alleviate some of the weight she had been carrying about with her since her visit to Samuel Davidson. No one could really help her, but it *would* be a relief to talk to an impartial listener.

'I'm not sure I know where to begin,' she said hesitantly, lowering her eyes to her hands in her lap to avoid his keen glance.

'At the beginning. It's always the best place to start, I've found.'

A nervous smile plucked at her lips, but she obeyed instantly, telling him everything as she had told Samuel Davidson, and ending with the bombshell that the loan was to be discontinued.

'Have you discussed the matter with your aunt?' Daniel Grant asked when she lapsed into silence.

'No, I haven't, and I don't intend to. Aunt Irene has always walked about with her nose in the air, and, because my father was nothing more than a clerk in the Civil Service, they were never made very welcome in her home.' Joanne stopped to draw a quivering breath. 'I'm surprised she tolerated having Bruce in her home those first three years while he was still at school.'

'Perhaps I should go and speak to the lady in an effort to make her change her mind.'

'It won't do any good,' Joanne said tersely, 'and I have no intention of begging.'

Daniel Grant's eyes narrowed slightly. 'This is no time to let your pride stand in the way of your brother's future.'

If he had slapped her it could not have had a more startling effect, and her eyes widened in her pale face. 'You're right, of course. It *is* pride that's preventing me from approaching her, but I don't think I would be able to take her refusal without feeling that I've belittled myself in her eyes.'

'Then I shall go and see her for you.'

Joanne was not too sure whether she should take him seriously or not. For Daniel Grant to intervene on her behalf was totally irrational. Why on earth should he take it upon himself to help her out of her predicament when it really did not concern him personally at all? She would have understood his anger at her negligence in the theatre, but not this sudden desire to involve himself in her personal affairs.

They had finished their coffee and Dr Grant drove her back to her flat in silence. It had been kind of him to listen to her problems, she thought distractedly, but it was foolish of him to think that he could help, and she was certain that his silence meant that he had realised this.

She directed him to her flat and, when he parked his car at the entrance, he addressed her for the first time since leaving the coffee bar. 'Give me your aunt's address.'

Joanne's hand tightened on the door handle. 'You're not serious about seeing her on my behalf, are you, Dr Grant?'

His expression hardened. 'Sister Webster, I never make statements I don't intend to fulfil, now give me that address and don't argue.'

Joanne gave him the address without further argument and he scribbled it down in his notebook. 'Will you give me a ring and let me know what she said?'

'I'll do better than that,' he announced briefly as she slid from the car. 'I'll come back here and tell you personally, so have a couple of sandwiches waiting, because I'm bound to be hungry.'

Joanne stepped back hastily as the car pulled away from the curb, but she stood for some time staring after him with a nervous flutter rising from her stomach. Really, she thought, the man had a nerve ordering her to prepare sandwiches for him as if they were still in the confines of the hopital where he might have had every right to do so!

She hurried up to her flat, and only as she closed the door behind her did she realise exactly what his order would entail. He would be coming up to *her* flat; her drab, sparsely furnished flat of which she was beginning to feel more than a little ashamed. What would he think? A man like Dr Daniel Grant, always so immaculate, and so obviously wealthy, had no place in her drab little world, and she had even less right to expect him to sit down and have a meal with her.

'Oh, lord,' she thought, removing her starched cap and taking the pins from her hair to let it fall loosely about her shoulders. 'I shall die of shame when he walks in here.'

Pulling herself together with an effort she went through to the bathroom to wash and change into a cool summer frock, the floral design brightening her appearance considerably. It would not take Daniel Grant long to discover how right she had been about his mission being unsuccessful, she thought as she pulled a comb through her golden-brown hair and applied fresh make-up. He would soon be back, and the sandwiches he had ordered had better be ready, or it would put the seal on her embarrassment.

Less than an hour later she opened the door to Daniel Grant, the colour coming and going from her face as he stepped inside and swept the interior with nothing more than a perfunctory glance before he settled himself in the most comfortable chair, and stretched out his long legs.

'What's the verdict?' Joanne asked, finding her voice at last.

'I refuse to talk on an empty stomach,' he said abruptly, closing his eyes and signifying that he was awaiting the sandwiches he had ordered.

Smothering an exasperated sigh, Joanne went through to the kitchen and poured the coffee, placing it on a tray with the sandwiches before taking it through to the lounge. He opened his eyes as she placed the tray on a small table in front of him and, smiling briefly, he helped himself to the ham and tomato sandwiches.

'Aren't you going to eat?' he asked in surprise as she sat sipping at her coffee.

'I'm not hungry.'

'Nonsense! You're far too thin, and you need to keep up your strength.'

An involuntary smile plucked at her lips. 'Do I need strength to hear the result of the interview you had with my aunt?'

'You'll need your strength for the operating theatre tomorrow,' he said briskly, biting into his third sandwich. 'I shall be watching you like a hawk tomorrow, so watch your step, Sister Webster.'

Reluctantly, Joanne helped herself to a sandwich, but after the first bite she realised how hungry she actually was, and Daniel Grant watched with satisfaction as she helped herself to a second and a third.

Replenished and pleasantly tired, she placed her empty cup beside his on the tray and leaned back in her chair, crossing one beautifully shaped leg over the other. It had not been such an ordeal having him there after all, for he never gave the slightest sign that his surroundings irked him in any way. He had accepted her home for what it was, and she was grateful to him for that.

'You have beautiful hair, Joanne Webster.'

Her lashes flew up to reveal startled eyes that became shaded with embarrassment. 'I—thank you, Dr Grant.'

'Did you know that it flashes gold in the sunlight?' he asked, lighting a cigarette and narrowing his eyes against the screen of smoke.

Was he flirting with her? she wondered frantically. No, it could not be possible, but it gave her a strange feeling to know that Dr Daniel Grant, one of the most eminent plastic surgeons in the country, had observed her long enough to notice the colour of her hair.

'What did my aunt have to say when you approached her on my behalf, Dr Grant?' she counter-questioned, directing the conversation on to safer ground.

'I'm afraid that she was adamant about not continuing with the loan,' he said abruptly, his expression hardening. 'I've seldom met such a singularly selfish person in my life, but I made her understand very clearly that I was there against your wishes, and I left her in no doubt as to what I thought of her.'

Joanne held her breath, afraid to ask for details, and ashamed that Daniel Grant had had to go through that experience with Irene Webster. 'I'm sorry.'

'Sorry that I told her what I thought of her?'

'No,' she lowered her glance to the threadbare carpet. 'I'm sorry you had to suffer such an unpleasant experience on my behalf.'

The silence weighed heavily between them, then Daniel Grant extinguished his cigarette with a thoughtful expression in his disturbing blue eyes.

'I've given this matter quite a lot of thought on the drive to and from your aunt's house,' he began, leaning forward in his chair, resting his elbows on his knees, and rubbing his chin thoughtfully with one of those slender, capable hands. 'I have a proposition to make, one which I think will not only solve *your* problem, but mine as well.'

'I don't think I understand, Dr Grant,' Joanne said hesitantly, finding it difficult to think of a man in his position having problems that could equal the seriousness of her own.

Daniel Grant's glance flickered over her, settling finally on the nervous little pulse that fluttered at the base of her slender, graceful throat. 'I shall pay your brother's university fees.'

Joanne sucked her breath in sharply. 'I'm not aware that I've asked you for a loan, Dr Grant.'

'I wasn't offering you a loan, Sister Webster,' he contradicted harshly. 'I'm offering to pay for your brother's expenses in order to set your mind at ease, and in exchange for that you could do something for me to alleviate the problem I've wrestled with over the past weeks.'

A warning flashed through her mind, but she ignored it for the moment. 'In what way could I help *you*, Dr Grant?'

'You could marry me.'

CHAPTER TWO

'*You could marry me*,' he had said, and Joanne reeled mentally under the impact as she stared at him in stunned silence. She could not possibly have heard correctly. But yes, she *had*, and Daniel Grant was waiting for some sort of reply to his shattering request.

'You can't be serious, Dr Grant,' she managed eventually, her mouth so dry that she thought the saliva had dried up permanently.

'I've never been more serious about anything in my life,' he assured her in his abrupt fashion, his eyes never leaving her face.

Joanne's colour returned slowly. 'But you can't want to marry me! You hardly know me at all, and besides, I—we don't——'

'Love each other?' he filled in ruthlessly for her, watching the play of colour on her cheeks as she lowered her embarrassed glance. 'Love doesn't enter into this arrangement at all. Love is a fabricated emotion I have no time for in my life. It's a word used in place of desire because people consider that it sounds more decent. But rest assured, I don't *desire* you, Joanne Webster. What I'm offering you will be purely and simply a business arrangement which will last no longer than a year.'

If someone had placed a gun at her head and demanded that she should explain her feelings at that moment, she would not have been able to. She felt numb to her very fingertips, and curiously as if she had been reduced to the insignificant carpet beneath his expensive leather shoes.

'Perhaps if you explained,' she said in a voice barely above a whisper as her wide and troubled glance met his.

'My mother is dying of cancer,' he said without preamble, and with a new harshness in his voice that told her how deeply it affected him. 'There's nothing more we can do for her except try to alleviate the pain as much as possible. She has, at the most, a year to live, but I doubt it very much in the face of her rapid deterioration over the past two months. My mother, like most mothers, I suppose, has the desire to see me married before she dies, and lately it's become almost an obsession with her that I should find the right woman and settle down.'

'And you want me to marry you in order to set your mother's mind at rest,' she put in, grasping the situation suddenly. 'But it would mean we would have to lie to her.'

Daniel's lips tightened. 'I would go to any lengths to ensure that her last few months on earth are happy.'

'You must love her very much.'

A flicker of a smile touched his lips. 'I *care* for her very deeply, which doesn't quite mean the same thing.'

Joanne rose from her chair and paced about restlessly, clasping her arms about her as if she was afraid she would come apart. 'If I—if I married you, and—and after a few months your mother passed away, what then?'

'Our marriage will be annulled and I shall continue to pay your brother's university fees until he graduates,' he hesitated abruptly, adding: 'Without demanding repayment.'

It sounded tempting, but it was a tremendous decision to have to make. It involved not only Bruce's future but her own, and she was not sure that she could enter into a loveless marriage with Daniel Grant without being hurt in the process.

'Would you give me a little time to think about it?' she asked after a lengthy pause, stopping beside his chair.

'How much time do you want?' he demanded with a hint of impatience in his glance.

'Could I give you your answer tomorrow?'

Daniel Grant rose abruptly and Joanne, tall herself, found she had to raise her head considerably to meet his glance.

'I shall be operating at eleven tomorrow morning. Give me your answer when the operation is over and done with.' He strode towards the door in his usual abrupt fashion, then turned, his hand on the door-knob. 'Thanks for the sandwiches.'

The door closed behind him and Joanne dropped into the chair he had just vacated, the warm impression left by his body suggesting a certain intimacy that made her rise swiftly and remove the tray to the kitchen.

Sleep evaded her that night as she lay pondering his proposal. It was strange that she had never thought of him as someone who might have a loving parent tucked away somewhere, but then she knew very little about him and the way he lived outside the confining walls of the hospital. He seldom attended the hospital functions, and she still recalled her astonishment when he arrived unexpectedly at the last Christmas ball. He had joined Matron at her table and had danced a slow waltz with her. Then, to Joanne's amazement, she had seen him bearing down upon her from the other end of the hall, and there had been no escape from the hands which had pulled her to her feet and into his arms.

He had danced well, and she had followed him perfectly, but when the dance ended he thanked her politely, only to disappear from the ball as suddenly as he had arrived. He was the strangest man she had ever met, Joanne had concluded, and she still thought so, but she never dreamt that he would one day come to her with such an outrageous proposal of marriage.

Marriage! The word struck a discordant note in her mind. How could she marry him and take those sacred vows with the knowledge that she was about to live a lie? It was contrary to all that she had hoped for and everything she had dreamed of in her twenty-four years. Every woman wanted a husband, a home, and children, so why should she be any different? She needed to love and be loved just as much as anyone else, but this marriage to Dr Daniel Grant had nothing to do with the usual reasons concerning such a union. It would be a business arrangement; a contract that would be signed and annulled soon after his mother's death, and for this service he would make Bruce's dreams possible.

'But what about my dreams?' she wondered, groaning inwardly. She could not do it, she told herself, but deep down she knew that she had no choice. Bruce's future lay wrapped up in her decision, and she could not let him down.

'You'll move heaven and earth to help me, but don't do anything foolish,' she recalled Bruce's parting shot, and here she was contemplating marriage to a man she knew only slightly for her brother's sake.

There was nothing really very complicated about Daniel Grant's suggestion, she told herself dispassionately as she stared into the darkness. It would be a business arrangement that would legally bind her to him for a few months until the contract was fulfilled, then she would be able to walk away a free woman, and with the knowledge that her brother would never need to look elsewhere for funds.

She was reasoning in circles, she knew. Her heart might reject the idea, but her mind had accepted irrevocably the proposal which had been put to her. All that remained was for her to give Daniel Grant his answer; the answer that would solve *his* problem, and her own.

Joanne glanced critically about the theatre. Dr Grant's patient would be the next to be brought in, and everything had to be in perfect order when Dr Grant walked in to begin the operation. There was to be no repetition of the incidents which had occurred the day before, Joanne realised, shutting her mind to everything except her work.

Daniel Grant was punctual, as usual, and he strode into the theatre at precisely eleven o'clock, but there was nothing in his manner towards Joanne that gave any indication of what had occurred between them the previous day. He was his usual abrupt self, which made it easy for Joanne to follow suit and, from the moment she slapped the first instrument into his palm, her mind was solely on her job.

She watched with fascinated admiration as those clever hands performed the intricate task of restoring a woman's badly scarred features, marvelling at the steadiness of his fingers as he stood for hours, tirelessly remodelling a nose and doing the necessary skin grafts. When the operation was finally over she knew, without being told, that he had notched up another success.

'I've ordered tea to be sent to my office, Dr Grant,' Joanne told him as he pulled down his mask and removed his surgical gloves, her glance lingering on his hands as he flexed those slender fingers to ease away the stiffness after the hours of surgery.

'Right,' he said without glancing up. 'Give me five minutes.'

Now that the moment had come, Joanne was nervous and apprehensive, doubting her decision and wishing herself a million kilometres away. It was too late, however, to change her mind, for the tea she had ordered arrived moments before Dr Grant, immaculate in his grey suit which accentuated his muscular slimness, entered her office.

Joanne marvelled at the steadiness of her hands as she poured the tea and passed him his cup, but Daniel Grant seemed quite unperturbed as he lowered himself on to the edge of her desk and drank his tea. He was a man of few words, and his silence had never troubled her before, but on this occasion she searched frantically for something to say; something to postpone the moment when she would have to give him the answer he was waiting for.

He must have sensed her discomfiture, for he brought matters to a head abruptly by saying, 'Let's get it over with, Sister Webster. What have you decided?'

She placed her cup and saucer carefully on the desk before her, swallowing nervously. 'Dr Grant, I——'

'Yes or no?' he interrupted harshly.

Their glances met and held, and Joanne heard herself say unsteadily, 'Yes.'

'Good,' he said, rising to his feet and placing his empty cup in the tray. 'I'll see you at seven-thirty this evening, then we can discuss the details.'

He was gone before Joanne could think of anything further to say, and she covered her face with her hands to stem her rising hysteria. She had just agreed to marry

Dr Daniel Grant, and all he could say was, 'I'll see you this evening, then we can discuss the details.'

What had she expected? she wondered, pulling herself together. This was no ordinary marriage they were planning, and there was no excited flush of happiness at the thought of becoming his wife.

His *wife*! The word shocked through her like an electric current. What had she done?

Bruce's face swam before her eyes, giving her her answer in no uncertain terms. She could not let him down. Not now, not ever!

Daniel Grant arrived at her flat that evening at seven-thirty sharp, and he wasted no time in getting down to business.

'Contrary to what you might have thought, Joanne, I don't intend to rush you through a quick ceremony in the Magistrate's office. To make it seem authentic, we shall become engaged, and the wedding will take place in a church with all the usual nonsense.'

Joanne paled visibly. 'You—you mean it's to be a white wedding with a reception and—and everything?'

His glance narrowed. 'My mother wouldn't settle for less than that.'

'When is the wedding to be?' she asked resignedly.

'Three weeks from this coming Saturday.'

'So soon?' the words were out before she could prevent them, and his angry glance made her shrink inwardly.

'There isn't time to waste,' he said bluntly. 'I'll make all the necessary arrangements. All you have to do is hand in your resignation tomorrow, and buy yourself a wedding dress.'

Resigning from her profession was something she had

not considered, and the thought filled her with obstinacy. '*Must* I resign? Surely I could go on working after we're m-married?'

Daniel Grant gestured impatiently. 'It's unethical for a husband and wife to continue working in such close proximity, and neither will I permit it. As my wife you will remain at home until there's no longer a necessity for you to remain there.'

She knew only too well that he was referring to the time when his mother would no longer be there, and she was filled with an intense curiosity to meet the woman Daniel Grant loved so deeply.

'Now, as far as your brother is concerned,' he interrupted her thoughts, 'does he have a bank account anywhere?'

'Yes,' she murmured, giving him the name of the bank.

Daniel jotted down the name. 'I shall contact them tomorrow and make arrangements for a certain amount to be paid into his account twice yearly. You can explain to him where the money comes from, if you like, but I must ask you to keep the actual reason for our marriage to yourself.'

'I realise that, of course,' Joanne admitted, staring down at her hands. 'If Bruce ever found out that I was entering into a bogus marriage for his sake, he would never touch a cent of your money.'

'Now that we have that sorted out, the only thing that remains is to buy you an engagement ring,' he announced, rising to his feet. 'Get your coat or something, we're going out.'

'Where are we going?' she asked in astonishment.

'To buy the ring, naturally.'

'At this hour?' she questioned disbelievingly.

A flicker of a smile played about his lips. 'I have a friend waiting at his shop this minute to show us his selection of rings.'

Joanne shrugged helplessly and went through to her room to collect a light summer coat. Daniel Grant certainly did not believe in wasting time, she thought as she slipped her arms into the sleeves and checked her appearance in the mirror. Her face looked pale, and she pinched her cheeks absently in an effort to regain some colour before she rejoined Daniel in the lounge.

It was going to be the strangest marriage she had ever imagined, Joanne thought as she sat beside him in his car while they drove to the centre of the city. It was like playing a game; a game of pretence, and the result would have to be convincing for the sake of his mother—and Bruce.

'Here we are,' Daniel said, parking the car at the entrance to a well-known jeweller. 'I can see Richard waiting inside for us.'

It was all at once like a nightmare, and she somehow found herself seated beside Daniel with a tray containing the most exquisite diamond rings in front of her. Their sparkle mocked and dazzled her into a hypnotic state that made it impossible for her to carry out Daniel's order to choose one.

'They're all so—so beautiful,' she managed at last, her glance pleading as it met Daniel's. 'Perhaps if—if you would choose one?'

'If you'll permit me, Dr Grant,' the man Daniel had called 'Richard' intervened apologetically, his dark glance resting speculatively on Joanne. 'Your fiancée hasn't the colouring for the usual white diamond. She needs something with a little more warmth and character to match her appearance.'

Daniel turned slightly towards Joanne, his glance sliding over her systematically until her cheeks flamed with embarrassment. 'You're right, Richard, and I think I know exactly which one would suit her best.'

Without hesitation, Daniel removed a ring from the tray and, taking her cold hand in his, he slipped the ring on to her finger. It was the most magnificent yellow diamond Joanne had ever seen, and it was set between two smaller diamonds of a similar colour. The fit was perfect as it sparkled on her finger beneath the light, and her throat tightened curiously when she thought of the exorbitant price Daniel would have to pay for a ring which was merely part of a game of pretence.

'Please, it's—it's far too expensive,' she managed to choke out the words.

'Do you like it?'

'It's beautiful, but——'

'Then it's yours,' he said abruptly, nodding to Richard.

The trays were deftly removed and the transaction was completed while Joanna remained seated where she was, unable to take her eyes off the ring Daniel had placed so carelessly on her finger.

'May I wish you and your future wife every happiness, Dr Grant,' the man said, bowing slightly.

'Thank you, Richard,' Daniel said calmly, drawing Joanne to her feet. 'We appreciate your good wishes, don't we, darling?'

Darling. The way he said it, it sounded so absolutely natural, she thought as she murmured a reply, but they both knew that it was merely for the benefit of the jeweller who observed them so closely.

When they were alone once more, driving through the busy streets, Joanne voiced her disturbed thoughts. 'Dr Grant, I feel terrible about accepting such an expensive ring. Our marriage——'

'Our marriage must appear as normal as possible,' he interrupted smoothly. 'If I'd placed a ring of inferior quality on your finger, my mother would be instantly suspicious, and so, I'm sure, would Bruce.'

That was so, of course, but it offered her little comfort as she sat there silently beside him, the unfamiliarity of his engagement ring on her finger forcing her to face the reality of the situation.

'Where are you taking me?' she asked nervously when she realised he had passed the turn-off to her flat.

'My mother is waiting at home to meet you,' he told her calmly, and Joanne tensed instantly beside him, glancing down at her plain cotton frock and rather drab coat.

'You could have warned me, Dr Grant,' she accused him with a touch of anger in her voice.

'To have warned you would have made you more nervous than you already are,' he replied calmly. 'And I think it's about time you start calling me Daniel.'

Alarm flashed through her. 'I—I couldn't!'

'You'll have to,' he commanded without taking his eyes off the road. 'Start practising now.'

Joanne's throat tightened. 'Habit dies hard.'

'Say that again, but this time add my name to it,' he persisted ruthlessly, and Joanne had the strangest notion that he was deriving a certain amount of amusement out of this situation.

'I hate repeating myself, but I will admit that it won't be easy breaking through the barrier of hospital protocol,' she replied finally, glancing at him as she added a hesitant, 'Daniel.'

'That's better,' he laughed briefly. 'It will come easier each time you use it.'

Joanne sat silently beside him, realising eventually that they were approaching Constantia, where Dr Grant's lovely gabled home was barely visible from the road as it stood among the oak and silver trees. When they eventually drove through the wrought-iron gates and up the circular driveway towards the large, imposing house, Joanne was barely able to control the shaking of her limbs. She had not been so nervous since that first time she had sat in on an operation as a student nurse.

'I don't suppose it's necessary for me to remind you that we shall have to indulge in a little play-acting?' Daniel remarked as he switched off the engine and turned towards her, his head and shoulders a dark silhouette against the night sky.

'I'll do my best,' she promised.

'You'll have to do a little more than your best,' he warned. 'My mother may be ill, but she's still very perceptive, and I want her totally convinced.'

'I shan't let you down, Dr Grant—Daniel,' she corrected, her cheeks flushed with embarrassment as she heard him laugh softly to himself.

The air was cool and filled with the scent of frangipani as they stepped out of the car, and Joanne stood for a moment, drawing on her training as a nurse to gain the necessary composure to face the ordeal ahead of her.

'This way,' said Daniel, taking her arm and leading her up the shallow steps towards the heavy oak door with its ornamental brass knocker.

In the large, dimly lit entrance hall with its two stinkwood chests, Joanne drew back nervously. 'Daniel ... do I look all right?'

'No, you don't,' he said abruptly, the gleam of mockery in his eyes making her realise that she had phrased her question badly. 'You're far too pale, but I shall remedy that.'

His hand grasped her chin firmly and, before she had time to guess his intentions, his mouth had fastened on to hers. Caught off guard, she kissed him back, her heartbeats quickening as she felt his hand in the hollow of her back drawing her closer until their bodies touched. This was not their agreement, she decided in a moment of panic, raising her hands to his chest and pushing him away roughly.

'That was uncalled for,' she accused angrily.

'Perhaps,' he agreed, his eyes on her flushed cheeks, 'but you're beginning to look more like someone who's just become engaged. Come!'

He caught her hand in his and drew her towards a door leading off to the right. He opened it without knocking, then, placing a careless arm about her shoulders, he drew her into what was obviously the living-room.

Joanne was all at once aware of several things; the heavy gold drapes hanging down to the floor at the windows, the marble fireplace with the ornamental brass clock on the mantelshelf above it, and an elderly nurse hovering over a frail-looking woman seated on the Louis XV-style sofa.

'Mother,' said Daniel, his arm disturbing and protective about Joanne as he propelled her forward, 'I've brought my fiancée home to meet you. Joanne, this is my mother, and this,' he gestured towards the other woman, 'is my mother's nurse-companion, Sister Johnson.'

Serena Grant's skin was almost translucent, her blue eyes large and smiling in her thin face as she gazed up at Joanne. 'My dear, I've been longing to meet you ever since ... ' She hesitated briefly, glancing at Daniel. 'Ever since Daniel gave me the wonderful news.'

Her appearance awakened Joanne's sympathy, and something more. Recognition. But where had she seen this woman before? she wondered curiously. 'I've been looking forward to meeting you as well, Mrs Grant.'

Sister Johnson detached herself from Mrs Grant's side. 'I'll leave you for a while, but don't overtire yourself.'

'Stop fussing, Sister Johnson,' Mrs Grant said irritably. 'I'm perfectly capable of taking care of myself.'

'It's already thirty minutes after your bedtime,' Sister Johnson warned, taking her employer's show of temper in her stride.

'Yes, yes,' Serena Grant gestured impatiently with her hands. 'Go and do whatever it is you do when I'm safely tucked up in bed, and stop ordering me about as if I were a child.'

'I merely mentioned——'

'It's all right, Sister Johnson,' Daniel intervened swiftly. 'Just this once we'll slacken the rules, but we shan't keep her longer than another half hour.'

Sister Johnson nodded agreeably. 'Very well, Dr Grant.'

'That woman is going to drive me insane, I tell you,' his mother complained the moment they were alone, and Joanne found it difficult to suppress a smile.

'Nonsense, Mother,' Daniel reprimanded gently. 'You just love having someone around to fuss over you, and you'd be miserable if she left. Admit it.'

'I'll do nothing of the sort,' she said haughtily, amusement lurking in her glance as she patted the space beside her on the sofa. 'Come and sit here beside me, Joanne, and you, Daniel, draw up a chair so that I can look at you both without straining my neck. Now,' she said, taking

Joanne's hand once they were seated, 'let me see your ring. Ah, yes, you made the right choice, child.'

'Daniel made the choice, Mrs Grant,' Joanne admitted, finding it surprisingly easy to use his name.

'Then I'm glad to see that he had sense enough to select something that suited you, my dear,' the grey-haired woman stated her approval, and Joanne's glance went swiftly to Daniel. 'When is the wedding to be?'

Joanne's mouth went dry, and Daniel stepped swiftly into the breach. 'We've decided not to wait longer than three weeks, Mother.'

Three weeks, Joanne thought. Three weeks of freedom before she became Daniel Grant's wife. His wife for a year, perhaps, but not for ever.

CHAPTER THREE

'WE must celebrate your engagement, Daniel,' Serena
Grant insisted, clasping her hands excitedly against her
breast. 'There's a bottle of champagne on ice in the
kitchen. Be a dear boy and fetch it.'

'You think of everything, Mother,' he laughed briefly
as he rose to do her bidding.

The moment he left the room, Mrs Grant turned her
attention to Joanne. 'My dear, I've waited so long for
Daniel to take a wife, and I was beginning to despair
that I would never have the pleasure of knowing my
daughter-in-law.'

'Mrs Grant, I——'

'I know I haven't long to live, Joanne,' Serena Grant
interrupted calmly, fingering the single string of pearls
about her neck. 'Knowing this has made it all the more
important for me to see my son happily married before
I go. You may think me an extremely silly old woman,
but——'

'I understand, Mrs Grant,' Joanne interrupted hastily,
suppressing her feelings of guilt, and finding herself
drawn towards this frail woman beside her. Where had
she seen her before? 'Mrs Grant—forgive me, but—
have we met somewhere before?'

The thin bony hand tightened momentarily on the
pearls. 'I don't think so, child. I seldom forget a face.'

Daniel came in at that moment with the bottle of champagne and three glasses on a tray, and they lapsed into

silence as he placed it on a low table close to the sofa.

'Don't get a fright,' he warned as he removed the silver wrapping and eased off the cork. It popped loudly, and the next moment the cork dropped into Joanne's lap.

'How wonderful!' Mrs Grant exclaimed delightedly. 'That means your first child will be a boy.'

'That's superstitious nonsense, Mother, and you know it,' Daniel accused gently, his glance resting on Joanne who wished the floor would open up beneath her. 'Besides, you're embarrassing Joanne.'

'Rubbish!' his mother argued. 'Doctors and nurses are never embarrassed. They work every day with human bodies and their various functions.'

Joanne recovered swiftly, depositing the cork on the low rosewood table as she turned to meet the humorous glance of the woman beside her. 'Outside the hospital walls we're just as vulnerable as anyone else, and just as susceptible to embarrassment.'

Serena Grant's steady glance never wavered as she nodded her approval. 'I think I'm going to like you, Joanne, and you must come and visit me whenever you have time off from work.'

'I would like that very much, Mrs Grant,' Joanne agreed with a rush of warmth.

'Your champagne, Mother,' said Daniel, placing her glass in her hand, then, drawing Joanne to her feet, he picked up the two remaining glasses and handed her one before slipping his arms about her waist. 'To us,' he said briefly, touching the side of his glass to hers.

The bubbles tickled her nose as she sipped her champagne, observing Daniel's mother over the rim of her glass as she drank, and wishing with all her heart it had not been necessary to fool this wonderfully courageous woman into believing that their marriage would be a real one.

Sister Johnson marched in a few minutes later. 'Your half hour is up, Mrs Grant. It's time you were in bed.'

'Oh, really!' Serena Grant said exasperatedly. 'You're behaving like an over-zealous watchdog.'

'Now, Mother, you've been up much later than usual this evening, and you have nothing to complain about,' Daniel intervened with a gentle reprimand. 'You've met Joanne, and you've had your champagne. Now it's time you went to bed.'

'You all fuss too much,' Serena Grant complained.

'It's for your own good, Mother.'

'I know,' she smiled suddenly, allowing Daniel to help her to her feet. 'Goodnight, Daniel, and you, Joanne,' she extended a hand and Joanne clasped it between her own. 'Come again soon.'

'As soon as I possibly can, Mrs Grant,' she promised. 'Goodnight.'

Sister Johnson took over from Daniel and, taking Serena Grant's arm, she led her from the living-room.

'I think your mother is wonderful, considering what she must be going through,' Joanne remarked thoughtfully once they were alone.

'She's not the kind of person to let life get her down,' said Daniel, gesturing towards her empty glass. 'More champagne?'

'Dare I?' she laughed nervously.

'You have nothing to fear.'

'I never imagined I had,' she replied soberly as she watched him refill their glasses.

The situation was unreal, Joanne thought to herself as they sat drinking their champagne. The day before she

had been unattached, and had not the slightest intention
of marrying anyone, and here she was calmly sipping
champagne, an engagement ring weighing heavily on her
finger, and three weeks left to her wedding day.

She raised her glance to find Daniel observing her
closely. 'How old are you, Joanne?'

'Twenty-four,' she replied without hesitation. 'And
you?'

'Thirty-five.'

She had guessed his age to be somewhere in that
vicinity, but it was unusual to find a man of his age who
was still single. 'Have you never considered marrying
someone and settling down? Does your freedom mean so
much to you?'

His glance was mocking. 'I'm marrying you, aren't I?'

Joanne lowered her eyes to the glass in her hands,
watching the bubbles in the champagne rise to the surface
and disintegrate as she said: 'This is different.'

'Yes,' Daniel agreed harshly. 'You needed the money
to pay your brother's university fees, and I needed a wife
to satisfy my mother's whim. It's not a very good basis
for a marriage, is it?'

Joanne winced inwardly, wondering why the truth
should hurt so much. 'Our kind of marriage doesn't need
a solid basis when we don't intend to continue with it.'

Daniel's lips tightened. 'Have you told Bruce yet?'

'No, not yet,' she replied, wondering distractedly how
her brother would take the news of her marriage. 'I'll ask
him to come round to my flat tomorrow evening.'

'Would you like me to be there with you when you
tell him?'

'I would rather tell him myself,' she said, surprised at
his offer. 'But I think it's an ideal opportunity for you

to meet each other. I'll ask Bruce to be there at seven. Would you give us half an hour alone together before you arrive?'

'Very well,' Daniel agreed abruptly. 'Drink up and I'll take you home.'

Joanne's thoughts revolved around Serena Grant as Daniel drove her back to her flat, and she experienced a stab of guilt on each occasion when she called his mother's image to mind. She wanted her son happily married before she died, but if only she knew what a farce this marriage would be. Her blue eyes, so like Daniel's, had been trusting and content, with a hint of sadness lurking in their depths. Her displays of temperament were merely a cover, Joanne had realised soon enough. It stemmed from a determination to avoid sympathy, while she kept to herself the painful knowledge that her time was so incredibly short.

She was a woman with character and determination, and they were planning to deceive her, Joanne realised with clarity as Daniel unlocked the door to her flat and switched on the light in the small entrance hall.

How could she marry him now when her conscience forbade it? 'Dr Grant, I——'

'Daniel.'

'Daniel,' she conceded, gesturing helplessly with her hands. 'I feel dreadful when I think of how we intend to deceive your mother. It seemed logical in theory, but now that I've met her, I—I can't go through with it. I *can't* marry you! The whole idea was ridiculous, and I——'

'It's too late to pull out now,' he cut in icily.

'You could explain,' she offered lamely.

'You saw her this evening, Joanne,' he said abruptly. 'You witnessed her happiness. Could *you* tell her now that it was all just a set-up?'

'No, I couldn't,' Joanne whispered, lowering her glance.

'And what about your brother?' Daniel pointed out ruthlessly. 'Where would you get the money to see him through university?'

'I—I don't know, I——'

'Joanne!' His hands gripped her shoulders, making her aware of their strength, and the faint but tantalising smell of his after-shave lotion. 'Don't let me down.'

'I'm sorry. It's nerves, I suppose,' she sighed, realising only too well that the happiness of two people depended on their marriage.

'You'll feel better about it in the morning,' Daniel assured her. 'Goodnight.'

Joanne's resignation was placed into Matron's hands early the following morning, and by that afternoon it seemed that the entire staff of the General Hospital knew of Joanne's engagement to Daniel Grant. The news had exploded along the hospital grapevine with such speed that Joanne had been rendered speechless when she found herself confronted by a few of her friends.

'We had no idea there was a romance blooming right under our noses,' they said. 'We never had a clue, but how does it feel, knowing you're envied by almost every eligible girl in this hospital?'

Joanne muttered something witty which sent them laughingly on their way, but, deep down inside, she felt sick. By handing in her resignation, she had publicly declared the fact that she was to marry Daniel Grant. To withdraw now would cause endless humiliation, and Daniel's expression, when he strode into her office during the course of the afternoon, told her that he was well aware of the fact that she had bound herself securely by her own actions.

'Seven-thirty this evening?' he confirmed their appointment brusquely, his glance cool and impersonal.

Joanne had risen to her feet, an automatic reaction when in the presence of a doctor or a surgeon, but Daniel gestured almost impatiently that she should be seated.

'It's all aranged,' she said, keeping her voice level. 'Bruce will arrive at seven, and a half hour is long enough to break the news to him.'

'Quite long enough,' Daniel agreed, his keen glance flicking her pale cheeks. 'If you want to look convincing, then I suggest you put some colour into your cheeks before he arrives this evening. I shan't be there on this occasion to kiss you into looking the part.'

With that parting shot he departed as abruptly as he had arrived, leaving Joanne with her cheeks flaming with embarrassment and anger, but she sensed a hidden warning in his remark. Bruce had to be left in no doubt that the marriage was being planned for the usual reasons.

Joanne had barely cleared away her supper dishes when Bruce arrived that evening. Dressed casually in denims and check shirt, he looked young and vital as he sprawled in a chair and waited for her to join him.

'You have news for me,' he said as she hesitated. 'I can see it written all over your face.'

'Yes, I have news for you,' Joanne admitted, keeping her left hand hidden in the pocket of her skirt.

'Don't tell me Aunt Irene has changed her mind!'

'No, she hasn't,' Joanne laughed nervously, 'but I've managed to obtain the money elsewhere.'

'From whom?' Bruce asked, his face eager as he swung his leg off the arm of the chair and sat up with interest.

'From my—my fiancé.'

'From your *what*?' Bruce exclaimed in surprise, his eyes mirroring disbelief.

'From my fiancé,' Joanne repeated with a calmness she was far from experiencing. 'That's the other item of news I have for you. I'm going to be married in three weeks' time.'

'I don't believe you!'

'It's the truth,' she assured him, extending her left hand towards him and allowing him to see her engagement ring. 'I handed in my resignation at the hospital this morning.'

Bruce fumbled in his shirt pocket for his packet of cigarettes, and lit one. 'I never even knew you had any-one special.'

'I don't always tell you everything about myself,' she fenced.

'Do I know him?'

'No, but you're going to meet him in a little while,' Joanne explained. 'He's Dr Daniel Grant, and he's a surgeon at the General Hospital.'

'How long have you known him?'

'I've known him for almost two years.'

'Is that how long you've been——'

'No, no,' Joanne interrupted swiftly. 'It's only just recently that we've been ... well, discussing marriage.'

Only very recently, Joanne could have added. The day before yesterday, to be exact.

Bruce observed her closely, his eyes narrowed against the haze of cigarette smoke. 'Jo, you haven't gone and done something foolish, have you? You're not marrying this man because of the money, perhaps?'

Joanne's heartbeats quickened nervously. 'Don't be silly!'

'You don't look like someone who's fallen madly in love,' Bruce persisted shrewdly, and Joanne wished frantically that Daniel would arrive to support her claims.

'What do you know about how people look when they've fallen in love?' she asked, making a lighthearted attempt at teasing.

'I've seen some chicks at 'varsity flashing their diamond rings about after becoming engaged, and their faces absolutely glowed with excitement and happiness.'

'I'm not a chick at 'varsity,' Joanne said sternly. 'I'm twenty-four, and at my age a woman doesn't go around flashing her ring to all and sundry and making a public exhibition of her happiness.'

'Maybe not,' he argued, 'but it's unlikely that they'd sit there looking as cool and calmly composed as you are.'

'Bruce,' she sighed helplessly, 'aren't you going to congratulate me and wish me happiness?'

'Jo ... this is for real? You're not just marrying this chap because of the loan?'

'No, Bruce, I'm not just marrying him because of the loan.' This, at least, was the truth, for she was also marrying Daniel for his mother's sake. 'And it isn't a loan, by the way; it's a gift.'

Bruce laughed cynically. 'If it's a gift, then it sounds very much like the *lobola* paid by a Zulu bridegroom to his bride's people, only this *lobola* is being paid in cash, not cattle.'

'Don't be facetious,' she said sharply as the doorbell rang. 'That will be Daniel.'

Joanne had never been more relieved to see Daniel than when she opened the door and stood aside for him to enter. Tall, and immensely attractive in a black blazer and grey slacks, he walked in, and her heart skipped a beat as he leaned forward and kissed her lightly on the cheek.

'Hello, darling. I'm sorry I'm late.'

'It doesn't matter,' she assured him swiftly, her cheeks stained a delicate pink as she turned and led the way into her small lounge. 'Daniel, I would like you to meet my brother. Bruce, this is Dr Daniel Grant.'

Bruce rose to his feet, but it was Daniel who took the initiative and stepped forward with his hand outstretched. 'How do you do, Bruce. Joanne has told me quite a lot about you.'

'Has she?' Bruce asked with a hint of sarcasm as they shook hands. 'Funny, she never told me anything about you until this evening.'

'Perhaps it's because I've rather swept her off her feet by my sudden proposal,' Daniel replied smoothly, turning to Joanne and placing an arm about her shoulders. 'Isn't that so, darling?'

Angry and embarrassed by Bruce's rudeness, she forced a smile to her lips as she glanced up at the man beside her and saw the warning glint in his eyes. 'I haven't yet got used to the idea myself,' she replied.

Bruce glanced from one to the other and made an obvious effort to pull himself together. 'Well, now that I have met you, Dr Grant, may I offer my belated congratulations to you both?'

'Thank you, Bruce,' said Daniel, lowering his arm down to Joanne's waist and drawing her firmly against his side. 'And make it Daniel, as we're soon going to be brothers-in-law.'

'About the loan——' Bruce began once they were seated.

'I'm not offering you a loan, Bruce,' Daniel corrected, seating himself on the arm of Joanne's chair.

'But I can't accept it on any other terms,' Bruce insisted.

Joanne leaned forward urgently. 'Bruce——'

'Just a minute, Joanne.' Daniel's hand came down on her shoulder and drew her back in her seat. 'If it would make you feel better, then consider it a loan, but I shan't press you for repayment. Do you accept?'

Bruce pushed a hand through his fair hair. 'Under those circumstances, yes.'

'Good,' Daniel said abruptly. 'I've already made arrangements for an amount to be paid into your account at the bank twice yearly. If you would just pay them a visit some time tomorrow then you can let me know whether the amount is satisfactory.'

Bruce's astonished glance met Joanne's briefly. 'Thank you very much. I can't tell you how much I appreciate your generosity.'

Daniel's hand slid from her shoulder with a natural ease until his fingers moved carelessly against her neck, creating sensations that made her tremble inwardly.

'Shall I make us something to drink?' she asked finally, desperate now to be free of his touch. 'Coffee?'

'Thank you, Joanne.'

His hand was removed and she escaped to her small kitchen with a heart that was behaving decidedly oddly as she switched on the kettle and set out the cups.

She heard the murmur of their voices, and saw Daniel lean forward in his chair as he spoke earnestly to Bruce, but Bruce remained sprawled in his chair, a look of disbelief on his thin, boyish face. Joanne could not blame him entirely for remaining suspicious. They had always been close, most especially these past five years, hiding nothing from one another, and sharing each other's hopes and dreams.

She sighed heavily as she poured the coffee, almost spilling some into a saucer as a deep voice directly behind her said : 'Need any help?'

She glanced nervously over her shoulder as she returned the percolator to the stove. 'No, thanks. I was just about to bring the tray through.'

Daniel's arms came round her from the back, preventing her from lifting the tray and turning her to face him at the same time. Alarmed by his nearness, she tensed inwardly, aware of his warm hands circling her waist, and the irregular beat of her heart.

'I'm afraid that Bruce isn't quite convinced,' he said in a lowered voice. 'He suspects our marriage has something to do with paying his university fees.'

Joanne moistened her dry lips with the tip of her tongue. 'What are we going to do?'

'I'm not too sure,' said Daniel, his eyes narrowed with thought. 'Can he see us from your lounge?'

She glanced swiftly in that direction. 'Yes, and he's looking this way.'

'Hm ... I think a display of affection might convince him.'

Her breath locked in her throat as he drew her into a close embrace. 'Daniel——'

'Put your arms around my neck,' he interrupted with a whispered command, his lips against her ear, his lean cheek hard and warm against her own.

'But I——'

'Do as I say, Joanne, or do you want your brother to think the worst?'

His lips against her ear sent little shivers down her

spine as she relented and did as she was told, but her hand somehow touched the back of his head to find his hair soft and springy beneath her fingertips. This was a situation she never dreamed she would ever find herself in; to be held in Dr Daniel Grant's arms, and to experience a strange thrill of pleasure as she felt his lips moving against her throat. The only thing that made sense at that moment was the realisation that she had to put some distance between them, and soon.

'Our coffee is getting cold,' she tried again, but her voice sounded strange to her own ears, and the unexpectedness of his lips against her own silenced any further protests she might have made.

'Be still!' she warned her heart at its erratic beat, while she forced her lips to remain passive beneath his. 'He's kissing you to convince Bruce, and not because he cares.'

'Break it up, you two, and bring that coffee!' Bruce's voice penetrated through to them, and Daniel released her with a convincing display of reluctance.

'Sorry, Bruce, we got a little carried away,' he said over his shoulder as he took the tray from Joanne and gestured with his head that she should go ahead of him.

With her heartbeats settling into a more comfortable rhythm, Joanne joined Bruce in the lounge, but, if nothing else convinced him, then the flush on her cheeks and the pinkness of her throbbing lips seemed to have the desired effect, for his smile mirrored relief as it met hers.

When Bruce finally announced that it was time he left, Joanne rose to accompany him to the door.

'Jo, you do love him, don't you?' he asked in a lowered voice, seeking complete assurance.

'Need you ask?' she managed with forced brightness.

Bruce shook his fair head. 'No, it was unnecessary.

One had only to look at you when you walked in from the kitchen to know how you felt.' His eyes twinkled with mischief. 'You looked just like those chicks at 'varsity!'

'Go before I throw something at you,' she warned laughingly, and Bruce hurried down the steps with a last wave of his hand, his canvas shoes making no sound on the concrete.

Daniel awaited her in the lounge, an unfathomable expression in his eyes as they followed her to her chair. 'Is he convinced?'

'Completely,' Joanne assured him.

'Pity,' he mocked. 'I was just beginning to look forward to another little session similar to the one we had in the kitchen.'

Joanne's pulse quickened, and she lowered her lashes to hide the disturbing emotions that rose unbidden to the surface. 'That isn't very funny.'

'I wasn't trying to be funny,' he assured her abruptly. 'You're a very attractive woman, Joanne Webster, especially when you leave your hair down the way it is now, and I wouldn't be human if I didn't experience some pleasure while holding you in my arms.'

She pressed her palms against her flaming cheeks. 'You shouldn't say things like that.'

'Why not?' he demanded, looking lean and muscular, and so completely in command of the situation. 'Because we're entering into a platonic marriage it doesn't mean that we must anaesthetise our natural instincts.'

'What—what do you mean?' she asked, frightened by something she could not put a name to.

A derisive smile twisted his lips. 'To put it bluntly, there's nothing in our marriage that says I can't admire your beauty, but you needn't fear that I shall make passionate love to you.'

Joanne wished at that moment that the earth would cave in beneath her, and it was with the greatest difficulty that she managed to sustain his glance. 'You're repeating yourself, Dr Grant. You made it abundantly clear last night that you don't desire me.'

'Just as long as we understand each other, and the real purpose of our marriage,' he said abruptly, rising to his feet as he spoke, and towering over her. 'Are you satisfied?'

Joanne nodded silently, unable to force a single word past her lips as she followed him to the door and saw him out.

Alone at last in her silent flat, she gathered her scattered wits about her like a cloak, shutting out everything except that persistent little voice that rose from within to haunt her. She fought against its insinuations as she rinsed the cups and left them on the rack to dry, but later, in the darkness of her room, she was defeated into admitting that she loved Daniel Grant; that for almost two years she had fought against this love, labelling it 'admiration and respect', and adhering to it with practised discipline.

Now, her defences rudely smashed, she experienced the pain and futility of her feelings for the man she was to marry. Perhaps, subconsciously, she had always guarded herself against this moment, but, by facing the truth, she had placed herself in a vulnerable position with nothing to shield her from the agonising realisation that, to Daniel Grant, she was nothing but the means with which to satisfy his mother's obsession.

CHAPTER FOUR

THE three weeks prior to their marriage passed with a swiftness that was alarming and, years later, Joanne was to look back on those weeks with a feeling of unreality.

On Serena Grant's insistence, Joanne moved out of her flat, and spent the remaining week in Daniel's home with his mother and Sister Johnson acting as chaperon. Released from her duties at the hospital, she had time to sell the odd bits of furniture she possessed, and to put the money to more practical use by buying a trousseau for the week she and Daniel were to spend their mock-honeymoon at his cottage close to Knysna.

Bruce involved himself in the wedding arrangements, realising the importance of the part he would have to play by taking their father's place, and generally endearing himself to Mrs Grant with his natural and still boyish charm.

During those last few days a surprising friendship developed between Daniel and Bruce. It puzzled Joanne and made her more than envious when she compared their easy-going relationship to the awkwardness that existed between Daniel and herself when they were alone; something which, whether by design or chance, seldom happened.

Joanne enjoyed the moments she spent alone with Serena Grant. She was a wise and clever woman, who seldom wasted time on platitudes, preferring instead the direct approach that kept Joanne on her toes.

'I'm glad you're marrying my son,' she admitted to Joanne one day after one of their harmless verbal battles. 'He's not the easiest man to live with, but you're not a fool. You'll cope admirably, my dear.'

Whether she would be able to cope or not made no difference, Joanne thought afterwards, for Daniel Grant would discard her like a worthless garment the moment his mother was no longer there.

On her wedding day Joanne was strangely calm and composed as she stared at her image in the tall mirror of the dressing-table. Her wedding gown of white embroidered silk, and her veil, made of imported Madeira lace, was Serena Grant's gift to her son's bride, and it was a gesture which had touched Joanne's heart deeply.

'This is my wedding day,' Joanne said to herself as she fingered her veil absently. 'I always imagined it would be the happiest day of my life, and here I am, less than an hour away from that wonderful moment, feeling as though this is someone else's day; someone else's wedding I'm about to attend.'

On the spacious lawn outside stood the marquee Daniel had hired for the afternoon, and the caterers were fussing over the last-minute details. But Joanne felt curiously detached from it all as she left her room and walked down the passage to the living-room where Bruce awaited her.

He looked unfamiliar in his dark suit with the white carnation in his buttonhole, and Joanne felt inordinately sorry for him at that moment as he fingered his collar nervously when he turned from the window at the sound of her step.

Bruce stared at her for several seconds, his glance travelling from the exquisite lace veil pinned to her golden-brown hair, down to her satin slippers. There was

an ethereal quality about her; a pureness that made her
an untouchable vision until the smile that began in her
eyes curved her lips humorously.

'Do you think Daniel will approve of the way I look?'

'Jo ...' Bruce shook his head as if to clear away the
cobwebs. 'You're beautiful.'

'Coming from my brother, that's quite a compliment,'
she said quietly.

'It's the truth,' Bruce replied, his throat working. 'I
wish Mom and Dad were here today to see you as I'm
seeing you. They would be more than proud of their
daughter.'

Joanne's throat tightened, but this was not the moment
for tears, or for thinking of what might have been. 'I
suppose Daniel and his mother have left for the church?'

'About fifteen minutes ago, yes,' Bruce nodded, running
a finger along the inside of his collar once more. 'Shall
we go? The car Daniel ordered for us is waiting, and we
don't want to be late.'

'It's customary for the bride to be late,' she reminded
him with a faint smile on her lips, but his apparent ner-
vousness forced her to relent. 'Perhaps it would be better
if we don't keep Daniel waiting. He's never been a very
patient man, and I can't see him being tolerant, not even
on his wedding day!'

Carrying a single orchid and prayer book, Joanne entered the church some minutes later on Bruce's arm. The
moment had come, and there was no longer any opportunity for a change of heart.

She became aware of several things almost simul-
taneously; the look of relief on Bruce's face at having
brought her this far without a hitch, the approval in
Daniel's glance as it arrested hers, and the warm pressure

of his fingers as he took her hand and placed it on his arm. Above all, she was aware of the intense happiness on Serena Grant's thin face, and the proud tilt of her head that forbade the tears that hovered on her lashes from spilling on to her pale cheeks.

It was for *her* sake now, more than Bruce's, that Joanne was marrying Daniel. She could not let this woman down; this woman who had accepted her fate so bravely and without complaint.

Joanne remembered very little of the ceremony that followed, recalling only the moment when Daniel placed the ring on her finger, and the feeling of panic which had assailed her momentarily. Then it was all over, and they walked out into the sunshine to be met by a sea of strange faces and a shower of confetti. She heard Daniel laugh and raise his hand protectively above her, cameras flashed, and then she was whisked off to a car and driven back to Constantia.

'Your mother,' Joanne said with sudden alarm as she turned towards Daniel in the back seat of the low-slung convertible.

'My mother and Sister Johnson will return with Bruce in the car that took you to the church,' he assured her abruptly, and Joanne lapsed into a relieved silence.

It was over, barring the reception, and that, Daniel had assured her some days ago, would not be dragged out unnecessarily, for he intended that they should leave immediately afterwards for his cottage.

Daniel's mother had invited over a hundred guests to the wedding, and the marquee accommodated them perfectly. Among the guests Joanne recognised some of the hospital staff, but in the confusion she never had a moment to have a word with one of them before Serena Grant whispered that it was time to change into something more comfortable.

Joanne went inside, thankful to escape for a few minutes, but Daniel caught up with her as she was about to enter her room, and her pulse quickened absurdly as he opened the door and followed her in.

'You look a little pale,' he said with a touch of concern. 'Are you feeling well enough to travel?'

'I'm perfectly well, Daniel,' she assured him, but he would not have agreed with her had he taken her pulse at that moment.

His compelling glance held hers for interminable seconds before he said : 'I've seen many brides, but never one as beautiful as you. I had to tell you now before you changed into something else.'

Joanne stared at him in surprise. How unlike Daniel to feel the need to compliment her, she thought, but instead she said; 'Thank you, Daniel. It's kind of you to say so.'

His expression was unfathomable as he inclined his head briefly and left the room, closing the door firmly behind him. How strange, Joanne thought. How utterly, delightfully strange!

There was no time to ponder over his behaviour as she removed her wedding gown and veil, and slipped into an amber coloured dress that enhanced the colour of her eyes. Through her open window she could hear the sound of the children playing beneath the oak trees on the lawn, their voices obliterating to some extent the noise coming from the marquee. Joanne only hoped that Serena Grant would not be too exhausted by the day's proceedings. She was not strong, no matter how much she argued to the contrary, and Joanne often came to the conclusion that it was her stubbornness that kept her going for such long hours on end.

'I shall miss the two of you,' Serena Grant announced when Joanne and Daniel went to say farewell. 'But don't hurry back on my account.'

'Is that an order, Mother?' Daniel demanded humorously.

'It is, and well you know it.' Her blue gaze softened slightly as she sat looking up at them. 'I never saw you kiss your bride, Daniel. It's customary for the groom to kiss the bride at least once during the marriage proceedings, and I'm surprised at you for neglecting to do so, considering what a beautiful bride Joanne made.'

Joanne's heart lurched uncomfortably, but Daniel took his mother's accusation in his stride. 'How remiss of me, Mother, but I shall set the record straight at once. Come here, Joanne. Your husband wants to kiss you.'

There, in front of Serena Grant, Sister Johnson, Bruce and several other guests, Daniel drew Joanne into his arms and placed his lips on hers, much to the enjoyment of everyone. It was a cool, impersonal kiss that left her unmoved, but, for the benefit of those watching, Daniel did not release her too soon.

'Satisfied?' he asked, smiling down at his mother while he kept his arm firmly about Joanne's waist.

'More than satisfied, Daniel. Now, be off, the two of you, and enjoy yourselves.'

Joanne kissed her soft cheek. 'Take care of yourself.'

'And you, my dear,' she smiled briefly. 'Be happy.'

Joanne turned away to hide the tears that stung her eyelids, only to find herself facing a forlorn-looking Bruce.

'You'll be back at the university when I get back, but

I'll telephone you at your flat one evening, then you can come over and have dinner with us.'

'I look forward to that,' he said, his lean face creasing into a smile that vanished almost instantly again. 'Jo, there were so many things I wanted to say to you, but somehow ...'

Joanne swallowed down the lump in her throat as she took his hand in her own. 'I know, Bruce. It's sometimes difficult to speak of the things that matter most, and you're all I have.'

'You have Daniel now,' he reminded her.

'Yes, I have Daniel,' she agreed quietly, 'but it's not quite the same, is it?'

Daniel gestured impatiently that they should leave, and Joanne planted a hurried kiss on Bruce's cheek before joining her husband. *Her husband.* How strange that sounded, she thought to herself as she climbed into the car and waved for the last time. Now they were alone, completely alone for a whole week, and heaven only knew how they would get the time to pass.

The drive to Daniel's cottage took several hours, and darkness had descended before they turned off the main road, heading for the coastal village of Salt Bay.

'We're almost there,' Daniel said as she stifled a yawn. 'I arranged with one of the locals to leave something in the oven for us when they went in to air the cottage and prepare our rooms, so we can have something to eat and get to bed early.'

'Didn't they think it strange that two bedrooms should be prepared when you're supposed to be on your honeymoon?' Joanne asked sleepily, blessing the darkness that hid her flushed cheeks.

'If they did, then they never mentioned it,' Daniel replied calmly, keeping his eyes on the ribbon of road illuminated by the car's lights. 'Does it trouble you what people think?'

'Not really, but——' She chewed her lip nervously. 'I was thinking of your mother. What if she should hear that—that we——'

'That we didn't sleep together on our honeymoon?' he finished for her with a bluntness that sent the colour rushing back to her cheeks. 'My father was several years older than my mother, Joanne, and they always had their own rooms. My mother wouldn't think it strange at all that we don't share the same room. She'll merely think I have the same preference as she and my father had.'

'And have you?' she could not help asking, stealing a glance at this formidable man seated beside her.

'No, I don't,' he said abruptly. 'I would want my wife in bed with me all night, and every night. I wouldn't agree to single beds either. Does that surprise you?'

'Not really,' she admitted, keeping her eyes in front of her. 'I think I should also want to—to——' She faltered with embarrassment.

'You would also want to sleep in your husband's arms?' Daniel questioned mockingly. 'Is that what you wanted to say?'

'Yes.'

'You may yet have your wish, Joanne. With someone else,' he added when he saw her start nervously.

'With someone else, but never with you,' she thought, wincing inwardly at the thrust of pain that held her silent.

Daniel's cottage was situated almost on the beach, a row of cedar trees making it quite secluded from the other cottages further along the stretch of sand. Caught in the beam of the car's lights, Joanne was afforded a glimpse of the thatched roof, the shuttered windows, and an ivy creeper making its lazy way along the one wall.

The interior of the cottage was not very large, consisting of a lounge, kitchen, two bedrooms and a bathroom.

'This will be your room,' he said, pushing open the first door to the left and placing her suitcase inside. 'I'll take the room at the back.'

His footsteps echoed further down the short passage as she stared about her, taking in the iron and copper bed with its multi-coloured bedspread that matched the curtains at the window. The dressing-table was an old-fashioned wooden one with several drawers, and a large mirror; the wardrobe was small, but large enough to accommodate the amount of clothes she had brought with her, and beside the window stood a marble-topped stand with an earthenware jug and basin placed neatly on it. The floorboards were polished and bare except for a small rug beside the bed, but the overall impression was pleasing. It was the ideal place to come to when one wanted to relax with the minimum of fuss, she thought, venturing into the lounge with its brick fireplace and padded green chairs.

Curiosity more than hunger drew her towards the kitchen, where she found a small table set for two, and a tempting stew waiting in the oven.

'Are you hungry?' that familiar gravelly voice asked behind her, and she swung round to find Daniel leaning with his hand against the door jamb, his jacket and tie removed, and a speculative look in his eyes.

'Not particularly. Are you?'

'No,' he said, coming towards her. 'But I suggest that we do eat something before we go to bed, or we might find ourselves awake around midnight, and starving.' He stretched out an arm and Joanne backed away involuntarily, the colour surging into her cheeks as she saw him raise his eyebrows mockingly. 'I'm taking down the plates, Joanne, nothing more than that.'

It had been a long day with unavoidable tension piling up within her, and the tears suddenly brimmed her eyes, spilling over on to her cheeks before she could check them.

Daniel swore softly as he put aside the plates and drew her forcibly against him. 'I can take plenty, Joanne, but not a woman's tears, and not on our wedding day.'

'I'm sorry,' she muttered, choking back her tears. 'I don't know what's the matter with me. I'm not usually this weepy.'

'We've both had a strenuous day, but you'll feel better in the morning.'

'Yes, I suppose so,' she agreed, the warmth of his body against her own, and the touch of his hand in her hair far too disturbing for comfort.

'Joanne,' her name sounded like a caress on his lips as he forced her face into the open. 'You have nothing to fear. I give you my word, just as I take your word for it that you'll do nothing to make my mother suspect the true reason for our marriage. You believe me, don't you?'

'Yes . . . I believe you, Daniel.'

'Good,' he said abruptly as he released her. 'Now, let's eat, and, if I'm not mistaken, there's a bottle of champagne in the refrigerator.'

Joanne dished up the stew while Daniel hunted for glasses and opened the bottle of champagne. The cork did not land in her lap on this occasion, but she found that she could laugh without embarrassment when he teased her gently about his mother's remark on that evening when they celebrated their engagement. Neither of them had been hungry, yet very little was left of the stew when they eventually piled their plates into the basin and sat down to another glass of champagne.

'Do you come here often?' Joanne finally asked out of curiosity.

'Whenever I get the opportunity, yes,' Daniel admitted, his eyes clouding. 'But I haven't been here for quite some time now.'

'Because of your mother?'

'Mainly, yes,' he sighed, staring down at the sparkling liquid he was swivelling absently in his glass.

The finality of his mother's illness was unacceptable to Joanne. 'Daniel, is there nothing——'

'If there was, do you think I'd sit back and allow the inevitable to happen?' he interrupted harshly, his eyes darkening with fury.

'No, of course not.'

'I didn't intend to snap your head off,' he remarked after a brief, uncomfortable pause. 'Of all people you should know just how frustrating it can be for a doctor when his medical knowledge is not capable of preventing a patient's death. You feel utterly useless, as though your years of study had been worthless, wasted time.'

'I *do* understand how you feel,' Joanne assured him, recalling the many occasions she had witnessed a doctor's desperate struggle to save a patient's life, draining his vast knowledge of medicine, and finding it inadequate in the end. 'It's just that knowing your mother, and knowing her courage, makes it so difficult to accept. And I hate the idea that we're deceiving her.'

'You couldn't hate it more than I do, but let's not discuss it further,' he brushed aside the subject and raised his glass. 'Shall we drink a toast to the future, and whatever it may hold in store for us?'

They drained their glasses in silence, but as Joanne moved towards the steel basin to wash the dishes, Daniel gripped her arm and steered her firmly from the kitchen.

'Leave them,' he ordered when she began to protest. 'You have all day tomorrow to be as domesticated as you like, but not tonight. Doctor's orders!'

A humorous smile plucked at her lips and, as they reached her bedroom door, she glanced up into his stern face and said: 'Yes, Doctor,' in her best theatre Sister voice.

Daniel smiled briefly and tugged at her hair. 'Goodnight, Joanne. Sleep well.'

Joanne switched on her light and closed the door, leaning against it for a moment. She felt curiously deflated, but, as her glance came to rest on her suitcase, she sprang into action and unpacked her clothes before going through to the bathroom. There was no key in the lock, but she hoped the sound of running water would warn Daniel of her presence.

She had had no reason to fear, however, for she had been in bed for some time before she heard Daniel's footsteps cross the passage and enter the bathroom.

This was her wedding night, she thought as she lay listening to the sound of the surf, but it was a wedding night with a difference. She was legally Mrs Daniel Grant, but her husband had no need of her as a wife in the true sense, while she—Joanne moaned softly as she buried her face in her pillow.

Why did she have to love him so much? Why did she

have to lie there wishing he would forget their stupid agreement, and come to her?

Alarmed at her own thoughts, she rolled over on to her other side, but Daniel's voice rang in her ears, taunting her cruelly. 'I don't desire you, Joanne Webster. I admire your beauty, but you needn't fear that I shall make passionate love to you.'

She raised her hands to her hot cheeks and was surprised to find them wet with tears. 'Oh, God,' she whispered into the darkness. 'Daniel must never know how much I care. I shall never be able to face him again if he should ever discover the truth.'

The wind came up and whistled through the cedar trees, and, on that hot February night, Joanne shivered, sliding deeper beneath the sheets as if to escape from the mournful sound that echoed what lay in her heart.

CHAPTER FIVE

DESPITE Joanne's misgivings, their stay at Salt Bay turned out to be a holiday she would always remember. Their days were spent on the beach, swimming, walking, or just lying on the golden sand to soak up the sun. She was beginning to know the man she had married in a totally different way. His abruptness gave way to a lazy mockery, and her senses had become sharpened at the sheer maleness of him, making her more aware of her own femininity than she had ever been before.

His mother's health became a subject they seldom discussed after that first night. It was almost as if they had both silently agreed that it was a forbidden topic, but Joanne's thoughts often dwelled on the woman she had come to love and admire in those few short weeks before their marriage.

She thought of her now as she stepped out of the bath and dried herself, wondering whether they would find her condition had remained constant during their absence.

A sound behind her made her turn, wrapping the towel about her with one hasty movement as she did so, while her heart leapt throbbingly to her throat.

'What do you want?' she demanded, fighting down a wave of panic.

Daniel, his one hand on the doorknob, and the other against the wall almost as if he barred her way, gave no sign of retreating as her bewildered glance registered the fact that he wore nothing but the briefest pair of shorts, while she wore nothing except the inadequate towel which she had to hold in position with her hands.

'I'm sorry,' he said unconvincingly, his eyes travelling down the length of her, and giving her the peculiar sensation that she had been stripped of her only protection. 'I thought you were in the kitchen seeing to the breakfast.'

'Would you mind going out again, Daniel, so I can get my clothes on?' she asked, keeping her voice level with an effort.

To her horror he closed the door and leaned against it with his arms folded across his tanned chest which was sprinkled liberally with short dark hair. 'I have no objection to watching while you change, and I'm in no hurry to shave either.'

His eyes flickered strangely and darkened, making her catch her breath sharply. 'Daniel ... please go!'

' He moved away from the door, but her hopes died a sudden death as he came towards her with slow, deliberate steps, making her heart hammer wildly in her breast as she sought desperately for escape. She had no way of guessing his intentions, and neither did she want to dwell on the possibilities which crossed her mind, but she felt decidedly faint as he reached out and drew the pins from her hair, letting them scatter on to the tiled floor while he pushed his fingers through her hair as it cascaded to her shoulders.

'Lorelei,' he mocked, his hands against her throat and sliding across her bare shoulders with a sudden possessiveness that made her tremble. 'You're nothing but a seductive water-nymph.'

'Daniel, don't,' she begged, but he gripped a handful of hair and forced her head back, and she was powerless to resist if she did not want to lose her grip on the towel wrapped so carelessly about her.

His hand was in the hollow of her back, drawing her against him unresistingly until she felt the warmth of his hair-roughened chest against the back of her hands. Her eyes were wide and pleading, but he brushed them shut with his lips before his mouth descended upon hers with a sensuality that broke through her paltry defences as he proceeded to coax her lips apart. She fought against the response clamouring within her, felt the hardness of his thighs against her own, and knew finally that she would have to make some effort to escape before she found herself submerged in sensations that sharpened to desire.

Grasping the towel with one hand, she used the other to lever herself away from him, while at the same time dragging her mouth from his. 'Let me go, Daniel!'

Her voice sounded hoarse and unconvincing, and his beard scratched her cheek as his lips sought the hollow behind her ear. 'Be still, Lorelei, and I shan't hurt you.'

His hands tugged at the towel and, fearing her own emotions more than she feared Daniel, she made a final effort to get through to him. 'You gave me your word!'

He drew back instantly as if she had slapped him, his face pale beneath his newly acquired tan. 'Get your clothes on, sea-witch. I'd better go into the village after breakfast to buy a bolt for this door, or I might be tempted to walk in on you again.' He strode towards the door and turned, casting a sardonic glance in her direction. 'I was wrong about you. When you're out of your starchy Sister's uniform, and with your hair let down, you're very desirable. So don't tempt me too much, Lorelei, or I might not keep my word next time.'

Joanne was shaking when he closed the door firmly behind him, but whether it was anger, or discovering the extent of her own emotions, she did not care to think as she hastily pulled on her clothes, zipping up her slacks with trembling fingers and tying back her hair into a pony-tail.

How *dare* he suggest that she had tempted him, when *he* had walked in on *her* without knocking, and had simply ignored her request that he should leave.

'Lorelei, indeed!' she muttered to herself angrily as she stormed from the bathroom, but her anger was accompanied by a flicker of pleasure. Contrary to his original statement, he *did* find her desirable, but desire was not quite what she wanted from Daniel Grant, and love was something he did not believe in.

Daniel went into the village after breakfast that morning as he had said he would, and Joanne, restless and uneasy after doing the few necessary chores, went down to the beach. It was not a day for swimming with the sky overcast and the wind blowing, but she rolled up her slacks to just below her knees, removed her sandals, and waded through the shallow water.

This was their fifth day at Salt Bay and there was still the week-end ahead of them, but Joanne was all at once in a hurry to return to Cape Town. She was being silly, perhaps, she told herself as she curled her toes into the cool wet sand, but her uneasiness had begun the day before, and she seemed unable to shake it off.

She walked on, past a group of children playing games on the sand, and on to where the rocks jutted out from the sea. A lonely fisherman stood on the rocks, throwing his line repeatedly into the angry-looking sea, but Joanne watched him absently, preoccupied with her own swirling thoughts, until she realised that she had been away from the cottage for longer than she had intended. Daniel would be back, and he would wonder what had happened to her.

Quickening her pace, she took the short cut over the sand dunes where a narrow path was marked out among the wild grass, but, with the cottage in sight, an involuntary cry escaped her as she felt a sharp sting beneath her heel. Going down on one knee to examine the injury, she was surprised to see the blood oozing from a small cut, caused by a broken bottle left by some careless person, and which had become embedded in the loose sand. Prising it out carefully, she threw it into the dense bush a few feet away and, admonishing herself for not wearing her sandals, she tried to stem the flow of blood with her handkerchief, her eyes filling with tears at the stinging pain.

She tried unsuccessfully to tie her handkerchief about her foot, and was considering hobbling back to the cottage when she looked up suddenly to see Daniel striding towards her across the sand, his grey slacks fastened with a broad leather belt about his narrow hips, and his blue shirt unbuttoned almost to the waist, displaying a tanned muscular chest.

'What the devil have you been doing?' he demanded as he reached her side.

'I went for a walk.'

'That's obvious,' he bit out the words as he kneeled down beside her. 'What's wrong with your foot?'

'I—I've cut it rather badly on a broken bottle.'

'Let me have a look.'

His hands were surprisingly gentle as he held her foot on his lap to examine the wound, but she winced at the

sharp pain that shot up her leg when he began to probe
it. 'There's too much sand in it at the moment to examine
it properly. I shall have to get you home so I can cleanse
it first.'

'I'll put my sandals on,' she said through clenched
teeth, but Daniel had other plans. He slipped an arm
about her waist and the other beneath her knees, lifting
her as if she were a baby. 'Daniel, put me down. Please...
I can manage.'

'To walk on that foot now would only cause more
harm, so put your arms around my neck, woman, and
stop chattering,' he ordered abruptly without halting in
his stride, and Joanne, flustered by his nearness, did as
she was told.

His breath fanning her cheek, and the hard warmth
of his body against her own, temporarily dulled the ache
in her foot as he carried her in silence, and with effortless
ease. His face was so close to hers that she could see the
fine wrinkles beneath his eyes, and the way his hair grew
back from his temples, soft and springy to the touch as
she had once discovered.

The hard steel of his arms tightened about her as he
kicked open the gate and walked up the path towards the
front door. 'Your hands are free, so will you open it?'

Joanne turned the door handle and pushed it open, but
Daniel did not relinquish his hold on her until they
reached the kitchen, where he lowered her into a chair
before fetching the first-aid box. He returned a few
seconds later and drew up a chair, lifting her foot on to
his lap as he gently cleansed the wound.

'This is going to hurt,' he warned eventually. 'I must
make sure that nothing stayed behind, so grit your teeth.'

Joanne nodded silently, closing her eyes and biting

down hard on her lip as he gently probed the cut. The perspiration stood out on her forehead when he eventually produced a tiny piece of glass for her inspection.

'It's fortunately not a very big cut,' she said in a voice that was slightly off key as he disinfected the area and applied a dressing.

'It's not very deep either,' he added, glancing at her white face. 'I'm sorry I had to hurt you, but it shouldn't take long to heal now.'

'I know,' she said thickly, fighting against the ridiculous tears as she bent down to ease on her sandals. 'It was silly of me to walk across the sand dunes without wearing something on my feet, and I deserved what I got.'

'Yes, you did,' he said without a shred of sympathy. 'But next time you will know better.'

Next time. There would not be a next time. Not at Salt Bay with Daniel, she thought disjointedly as she rose to her feet and tested her heel by carefully putting her weight on to it and, satisfied that it would not cause her much discomfort, she put the kettle on the stove to make a pot of tea while Daniel returned the first aid kit to its proper place in the bathroom.

It was at the luncheon table that day that Joanne could no longer keep her uneasiness to herself and, pushing her plate aside, she said : 'Daniel, don't you think it's time we returned to Cape Town?'

His glance was instantly mocking. 'If you would care to take a look, you'll notice that I've put a bolt on the bathroom door. Or are you afraid I might break the door down?'

'It isn't that,' she protested, blushing profusely under his close scrutiny. 'It's your mother.'

His expression altered instantly. 'What about my mother?'

'I don't know,' she admitted, lowering her glance to the checkered tablecloth. 'I wish I could explain, but I— I have had this awful feeling since yesterday that—that we should go back.'

Absolute silence greeted her remark, and for a moment she expected a rebuke before he said quietly, 'Is this what they call women's intuition?'

'Call it what you like,' she replied, raising her glance to his, 'but I can't rid myself of the feeling that something is wrong.'

Daniel's eyes narrowed slightly. 'I learnt during my first few years as a medical man that I should always take note when a nursing Sister has a hunch about a patient, or an intuitive feeling concerning their health.' He pushed back his chair and rose to his feet. 'I'll take a drive down to the Post Office and telephone home.'

'I'm coming with you,' Joanne said quickly, piling the dishes into the basin before she followed him out to the car. 'How would Sister Johnson have got a message through to you if your mother was seriously ill?'

'The switchboard operator at the Post Office has instructions to contact me the instant any such calls came through,' he said abruptly as he started the car. 'Knowing Mother, and how she feels about our spending this week on our own, I wouldn't be surprised if she instructed Sister Johnson not to let us know that she was ill.'

'Would Sister Johnson allow herself to be overruled in this respect?'

'Mother can be very determined if she puts her mind to it,' Daniel replied with a brief smile as the car picked up speed on the dirt road.

They seemed to reach the Post Office in no time at all, and Joanne remained in the car while Daniel went inside to use the telephone. She was beginning to have serious misgivings about her feelings of uneasiness. What if she had brought Daniel out into the village only to discover that her concern had been unnecessary?

Daniel emerged from the red brick building after what seemed an eternity, and from his tight-lipped expression she gathered that her intuition had been correct.

'Daniel?' she questioned anxiously as he climbed in beside her and slammed the door.

'Dr Erasmus has ordered her to bed for a few days after she collapsed yesterday morning. She wouldn't hear of Sister Johnson telephoning us, and as there was no immediate danger, Sister Johnson agreed.'

Remaining at Salt Bay until after the week-end seemed senseless in the face of Serena Grant's ill health, and Joanne herself put an end to their stay. 'If we leave immediately, we could be in Cape Town before dark.'

Daniel gazed at her intently for a moment before he nodded. 'Right! Let's get back to the cottage and pack. The honeymoon is over.'

They arrived at Constantia just after six that evening, and dusty and tired as they were, they left their suitcases in the entrance hall and went immediately to Serena Grant's room.

'Children!' Her eyes widened with surprise as they approached her bed, and Joanne felt a measure of alarm as she glanced at the painfully thin body in the lace nightie and bedjacket. 'Why on earth have you come home so soon?'

Sister Johnson excused herself politely as they kissed

Mrs Grant's pale cheeks and seated themselves on either side of the bed.

Daniel smiled at Joanne with convincing tenderness. 'My wife grew tired of having me under her feet all day.'

'That's not true, Mrs Gra—Mother,' Joanne stumbled over her words, still finding it strange to think of herself as Daniel's wife. 'We both decided that we wanted to spend the week-end at home with you.'

The clear blue eyes gazing up at them were filled with suspicion. 'Was Sister Johnson silly enough to disobey my orders? Did she telephone you and ask you to cut your honeymoon short on my account?'

'Why should she have telephoned us?' Daniel asked innocently.

'You know very well why, Daniel,' Serena said crossly. 'I was silly enough to faint yesterday, and here I am, trussed up in bed like an invalid, and hating every minute of it.'

'The rest will do you good, Mother,' he said, patting her hand reassuringly, but Serena Grant was not to be soothed.

'Rest? What rest do I get with that woman fussing over me all day with pills, and those dreadful injections. I'm beginning to feel like a pincushion, and I dare say Sister Johnson enjoys getting her own back on me by jabbing that needle into me.' She lay back against the pillows, exhausted by her effort, but with a gentle little smile playing about her lips. 'Oh, I can't say I blame her. I do tend to make life difficult for her, and she takes it all so calmly. Bless her!'

'That's quite a confession, Mother,' Daniel laughed, his glance including Joanne. 'Just wait till we pass this on to Sister Johnson.'

'I shall deny every word,' Serena Grant announced with a gleam of stubbornness in her eyes. 'Now, go and get yourselves ready for dinner—Oh, dear! I hope Violet has cooked enough. We didn't expect you till Sunday.'

'Violet normally cooks enough food to feed three families, let alone one,' Daniel remarked dryly, rising to his feet and gesturing that they should leave. 'We'll see you later, Mother.'

'Yes, later,' she agreed, closing her eyes. 'Joanne and I must still have a long talk. There's so much I still want to tell you, and so much I still want to know.'

Once outside the door, Joanne turned to Daniel. 'She doesn't look too well.'

'No,' he admitted with a frown. 'I shan't be surprised if she never gets up again.'

'Daniel, don't say that!' she whispered, alarmed by his deduction, yet knowing deep in her heart that he was right.

'Come, let me show you to our rooms.'

Daniel led Joanne to the north-facing side of the single-storeyed house where she knew the master bedroom was situated, and as they entered the large bedroom with its four-poster bed and white drapes, a nervous pulse fluttered in her throat. A bathroom adjoined this room, but it was the second door that caught her attention and held it.

'That will be my room,' Daniel told her, a flicker of mockery in his glance. 'As you can see, there's a key in the door, and you can lock it if it would make you feel any better.'

Joanne's cheeks grew hot. 'I never thought it would become necessary to lock my door against you.'

He turned towards her then, and she stepped back a

pace to avoid their bodies touching, but she found the foot of the bed pressing into her back as he placed a hand on either side of her face and raised it so that she was forced to meet his glance, and what she saw there was enough to place her on her guard.

'The trouble is, Joanne,' he said slowly, his thumbs moving caressingly across her cheeks, 'you're like a heady Cape wine. To take one sip is fatal, because you want to taste it again, and again.'

'Daniel, please!'

'Daniel, please kiss me?' he mocked, his breath warm against her mouth. 'You don't have to beg, my Joanne, because I want nothing more than to kiss you at this moment.'

'You know that isn't what I meant,' she said angrily, fighting against a weakness that threatened to overpower her as he held her against the foot of the bed with the weight of his body.

'You disappoint me,' he said against her lips, laughing inwardly at her futile attempts to push him away. 'When the fragrance of the wine tantalises the palate, then one has no option but to taste it, and savour it for as long as possible.'

His mouth descended upon hers, gentle at first, then with increasing passion until it was indeed like a heady wine racing through her veins, making her light-headed, and intensely aware of the warm maleness of this man who was now drawing her so firmly into his arms that there seemed no escape from the hard, muscular body that bruised her softness.

It seemed an eternity before he released her and stepped back. His face was an inscrutable mask except for the eyes that seemed to have darkened with emotion.

'I can tolerate your display of affection when we have an audience which must be convinced,' she said in a voice that was shaky. 'But I won't tolerate it when we're alone. You have no right to kiss me the way you do, and it certainly wasn't in our agreement.'

'There's no written agreement——'

'No, but I took your word for it,' she cut in swiftly. 'You did give me your word, Daniel, or can't I trust you to keep it?'

'I'm trying hard to keep my word, Joanne, but I'm a man, and I'm only human.' A cynical smile twisted his lips, and her heart. 'Legally, you're my wife, and that gives me certain rights. Can you blame me when there are times I can think of nothing else except the fact that you're a beautiful woman, and that you're rightfully mine?'

'I married you for your mother's sake.'

'And for a certain sum of money,' he retaliated harshly. 'Let's not forget that.'

'I'm not likely to,' she snapped, fighting against the helpless tears. 'I feel degraded enough at having to go to such lengths to get the money for Bruce's education.'

'Joanne,' he said at length, his hands gripping her shoulders painfully, 'let's stop ramming the reasons for our marriage down each other's throats.'

'It's *your* fault,' she accused in a choked voice.

'Because I kissed you?' he mocked her. 'I wouldn't have kissed you if I didn't know you enjoyed it just as much as I did.'

'I don't enjoy it,' she forced the words from her unwilling lips, for even now the touch of his hands had the power to quicken her pulse rate.

'Yes, you do,' he insisted, shaking her slightly. 'And

I'm beginning to think that if I went on to make love to you, you'd enjoy that as well.'

'How dare you!' she cried, twisting out of his reach and putting some distance between them.

Daniel pushed his hands into his pockets and rocked himself slightly on his feet as he glanced at her through narrowed eyes. 'I dare because every time I've kissed you it's sparked off a feeling of desire, not only in myself, but in you as well, and to deny it would be cowardly.'

The denial died on her lips as a tremor shook through her, forcing her to face the truth for what it was. If Daniel was determined enough she would have no resistance against his lovemaking, and it was not Daniel she feared so much, but the extent of her own emotions, and the lack of control she appeared to have over them.

'I don't deny the physical attraction between us,' she said at last when she found her voice, her cheeks stinging when she saw a flicker of triumph in his eyes. 'I feel, though, that it's something we should guard against and avoid at all costs. We married each other for reasons I shan't mention again, and it would be foolish to jeopardise our future merely because we're physically attracted to each other. We might both meet someone one day with whom we would want to spend the rest of our lives, and I could never give myself to a man purely for a physical reason. For a man it's different, I know. You could make love to a woman one day, and forget her the next, but for a woman, for me, it wouldn't be that way.'

He stretched out a hand and touched her hair, curling it about his fingers. 'No, it wouldn't be that way for you,' he said with a strange look in his eyes. 'You would give not only your body but your soul, and you would want nothing less in return.'

'Would that be asking too much?'

'No,' he shook his head, dropping his hand to his side a little wearily. 'I'll meet you in the dining-room when you're ready.'

As the connecting door closed behind him, Joanne passed a tired hand over her eyes. Why this conversation with Daniel had to upset her so much, she did not know, but she suddenly felt tired, and her foot seemed to be throbbing unmercifully where she had cut it that morning. She sighed audibly, pulling herself together as she lifted her suitcase, which must have been brought in by one of the servants, and started to unpack. Her other clothes had been brought from the room she had occupied before their marriage, and had been hung neatly in the wardrobe. The rest of her things, she found, had been neatly folded and placed in the drawers of the dresser, and on the dressing-table stood a bottle of perfume she had left behind, and some talcum powder.

She relaxed finally in a warm scented bath, allowing the tension to uncoil within her before she soaped herself luxuriously, and several minutes passed before she limped from the bath to the small stool to apply a fresh dressing to her inflamed foot. It would feel better in the morning, she decided, coming to the conclusion that she had stood on it too much that day, and that all it needed was a little care without any pressure on it.

Her thoughts inevitably returned to Daniel, and her body tingled as she recalled her treacherous emotions when he had kissed her. Physical desire, she had called it, but it was far more than that to her. It was the desire to love spiritually as well as physically, but it was the kind of love that would not interest Daniel for very long before he became bored with it, and went in search of someone else perhaps; someone who would not be fool enough to give her heart so completely, and would be solely in need of physical satisfaction.

'Oh, God, I did try not to love you, Daniel,' she moaned softly to herself as she went through to her room to change for dinner.

After dinner that evening she went with Daniel to his mother's room, but she did not stay long, and, pleading tiredness, she returned to her own room and went to bed. She could not remember when last she had felt so dreadfully tired, and her eyelids drooped almost before she had time to switch off the light.

Joanne slept fitfully, her dreams disturbing and frightening, but nothing tangible until she dreamt that she found herself trapped in the midst of a forest fire. Daniel stood beyond the circle of fire, his arms outstretched to help her, but although she called his name frantically she was unable to reach him.

She awoke with a sudden start to find Daniel bending over her, his hands on her shoulders forcing her back against the pillows. 'Take it easy, I'm only trying to help you.'

'Daniel!' she gasped, relaxing now. 'I had the most dreadful dream.'

'Yes, I know,' his deep voice reassured her. 'I heard you calling my name and I suspected you were having a nightmare.'

'I'm sorry,' she gulped, breathing heavily.

'You're feverish,' he remarked, touching her face with the back of his hand and sliding it down into her neck.

'I don't feel very well either,' she admitted, coming to her senses at last. 'My foot is throbbing.'

Daniel pulled the blankets aside unceremoniously to expose her right foot, and a muttered oath escaped him. 'When did the throbbing start? Can you remember?'

'Before dinner this evening.'

'Why the devil didn't you tell me?' he thundered at her, and she closed her eyes against the sudden rush of tears. 'Your heel is badly infected.'

'I didn't think it was anything serious,' she muttered, struggling up into a sitting position.

'Lie down,' he instructed harshly. 'I'll be back in a minute.'

He was gone for less than that and Joanne watched him fill a syringe from a small phial. 'Penicillin?'

'Yes,' he nodded. 'I'm going to give you a shot which should counteract the infection.'

With an efficiency she knew so well, he disinfected her arm and plunged in the needle, only to dab at the tiny mark seconds later. His fingers gently explored the cut before he applied a clean dressing, then, pulling the blankets into position, he stood staring down at her for several seconds.

'You'll feel better shortly,' he said abruptly. 'I'll leave my door open, so if you need me, just call.'

He did not wait for her to reply, and strode towards his room with his medical bag in his hand.

'Daniel?' He turned at the sound of her voice. 'Thank you.'

'I'll send you an account,' he said with a touch of humour. 'Goodnight.'

'Goodnight,' she smiled, switching off the light and settling down to sleep.

The door between their bedrooms stood open, but on this occasion Joanne found it comforting to know that he was near and, as the throbbing in her foot subsided, she slipped into a dreamless sleep.

CHAPTER SIX

SERENA GRANT'S health deteriorated with slow persistence during the weeks that followed, and it was as Daniel had forecast. His mother never did get up out of her bed again, for she became too weak to do more than sit propped up in bed against her pillows.

'Dear child,' she said one evening when Joanne drew up a chair and sat down beside her bed. 'I sometimes think that life would have been terribly boring without you to keep me company.'

'Nonsense!' Joanne protested, taking the thin hand between her own. 'You would have had Daniel and Sister Johnson to fuss over you and pamper you.'

'Daniel has his work that occupies so much of his time, and Sister Johnson does her duty admirably, but I would hate to be fussed and pampered.' Those blue eyes, still so remarkably perceptive, met Joanne's. 'You don't pamper and fuss me. You put me in my place, and smartly so. Ah, Joanne, that's what I like about you, and why I'm so happy with my son's choice. It would have been dreadful had he married someone I couldn't get on with.'

Joanne flinched inwardly. 'Daniel wouldn't have married anyone you didn't approve of, Mother.'

'Love is a funny thing, Joanne. It isn't always sensible, and Daniel has always had a mind of his own. My approval or disapproval would have made no difference to his choice of a wife.' Her hand moved a little in Joanne's. 'He married you because he loved you, and my approval was by the way.'

'He married you because he loved you,' the words echoed through Joanne. 'Oh, God, if only it were true!'

Serena Grant sighed and closed her eyes, but Joanne remained beside her until her regular breathing indicated that she was asleep, then, sliding her hand carefully from beneath hers, Joanne left the room quietly.

'He married you because he loved you,' Serena Grant's remark kept returning, and choking back the tears Joanne fled down the passage, only to cannon into Daniel as he emerged from his study.

'Where's the fire?' he demanded, his hands steadying her.

'Daniel, I must speak to you,' she said with an urgency that made him glance at her sharply before he drew her into his study and closed the door.

'What is it?'

'Daniel, I can't go on living this lie,' she choked out the words. 'We *must* tell your mother the truth. It isn't fair to let her go on thinking that we—that we're happily married. It isn't fair!'

'Pull yourself together!'

His voice had the effect of a whiplash, and she stared at him, pale-faced and trembling. 'I'm sorry. It's just that I feel so terribly guilty each time she talks about us, and she talks about us often.'

'Isn't that an indication of how happy it's made her to know that we're married?' he asked, placing a hand beneath her chin and raising her face to his. 'Do you want to take that happiness from her now when it means so much to her?'

Joanne drew a shuddering breath. 'I wouldn't do anything to make her unhappy, you know that. But it isn't a nice feeling to know that you're deceiving someone who has such trust in you. Every time she talks about us I feel like a criminal, and I sit there hating myself for lying to her.' She turned away and buried her face in her hands. 'I love and respect her too much to continue with this farce.'

'You must!' Daniel insisted, his hands gripping her shoulders painfully. 'You promised!'

'She doesn't deserve it, Daniel. Please!'

He turned her roughly to face him. 'Are you going back on your word?'

She sustained his glance for a moment, saw the angry determination on his face, and lowered her lashes in defeat. 'No, I shan't go back on my word.'

He released her with something of a sigh, and Joanne nursed her shoulders gently where his hands had bruised her soft flesh. If only she could make Daniel realise how wrong it was to deceive his mother in this way—but she knew that her efforts would be futile. She should never have agreed to this marriage in the first place, but she had been so desperate for the financial help he had offered, and ... she had loved him. She had selfishly not given Serena Grant a thought until it was too late. She had been caught up in the web of deceit, and there was now no way out except by telling the truth, but Daniel would never allow it.

Bruce came to lunch the following Sunday and remained for the rest of the afternoon. They had tea in the garden beneath the shady branches of the large old oak tree, and when they were left alone for a few minutes, he said:

'You don't look too well. You're not pregnant, are you?'

'Don't be silly,' she replied, flushing deeply.

'What's so silly about that?' Bruce demanded humorously. 'You've been married for almost three months, and pregnancies do happen, you know.'

'Not to me, it won't,' she replied instantly, but realising how that must sound, she added swiftly, 'Not now, anyway.'

'I always thought you liked children.'

'I do, but——' She bit her lip and sighed. 'Have another biscuit and stop being so personal!'

His green eyes danced with merriment. 'I just thought that you're not getting any younger, and——'

'Bruce!'

'Okay, okay!' he laughed, raising his hands defensively, but after a thoughtful silence, he said: 'Mrs Grant looks worse every time I see her.'

'She's going down rapidly now,' Joanne admitted, finding the cooing of the doves in the trees a little mournful.

'Daniel looks pretty low these days too,' Bruce observed, helping himself to another biscuit as she had suggested earlier.

'It isn't very pleasant for him to sit back and watch his mother slipping away from him.'

'I've an idea it's something more than that,' Bruce remarked thoughtfully.

His conscience, perhaps? Joanne could not help thinking. Since that evening when she had begged him to tell his mother the truth, the subject had never been mentioned again, but her guilt had become a festering wound inside her which threatened constantly to erupt.

That same evening, as Joanne and Daniel stood beside Serena Grant's bed in the dimly lit room, Joanne experienced again that feeling of guilt as Daniel's arm lightly circled her waist.

'I'll look in on you again later, Mother,' he said after a while, flicking back the cuff of his jacket to glance at his watch. 'There's a patient of mine I would like to call on at the hospital.'

'Of course, dear,' she smiled. 'Joanne will stay and talk to me.'

'You shouldn't tire yourself so, Mother,' Daniel said with concern.

'It's never tiring to listen to Joanne speak,' Serena Grant replied instantly. 'She has the kind of voice that's so soothing it would make the angels sit up and take notice. Don't tell me, Daniel, that you've never noticed?'

'Naturally, Mother. That's one of the reasons why I married her,' he replied, flicking a casual glance over Joanne's flushed cheeks. 'I'll see you later as well.'

His hand was warm against her side as he drew her closer and kissed her lingeringly. It was for his mother's benefit, she knew, but that did not prevent her treacherous heart from missing a beat, and when they finally heard his car going down the drive, Joanne could still feel the warmth of his lips against her own as she pulled up a chair and sat down beside the bed.

'Joanne, I know I can be an interfering old woman at times,' Serena Grant said tiredly, her hand searching for Joanne's and gripping it weakly. 'Is everything as it should be between Daniel and yourself?'

Joanne's heart lurched uncomfortably. 'What—what do you mean, Mother?'

'Oh, I don't know. It's silly. I suppose, but I sometimes get the feeling that something is wrong, and it troubles me.' Her shrewd glance saw the colour receding from Joanne's cheeks. 'There *is* something, isn't there?'

'No, no, of course there isn't.'

'Joanne ... you lie so very badly, and I'm not a fool. I love you as though you were my own daughter, so won't you confide in me?'

Joanne felt trapped between the desire to tell the truth, and the fear of breaking her word to Daniel. 'I can't! I promised——'

'You promised Daniel you wouldn't speak to me about it?' Mrs Grant cut in persuasively.

'Yes.'

The grey head nodded thoughtfully. 'Do you love my son, Joanne?'

'I—Yes, very much,' she admitted truthfully after a halting, embarrassed start.

'Ah ... then it doesn't matter that he rushed you into this marriage to satisfy my foolish desire,' Serena Grant sighed, and Joanne felt as though the floor had caved in beneath her.

'You—you know?'

'I suspected it, and you've just confirmed it,' the older woman admitted with a triumphant little smile playing about her lips.

'Oh, Mother! You tricked me,' Joanne rebuked her gently, realising that she had stepped neatly into the trap Serena Grant had laid for her.

'Yes,' she laughed softly and without the slightest sign of remorse. 'Terrible old woman, aren't I?'

'Never terrible,' Joanne contradicted. 'We just under-estimated you, that's all.'

Her hand gripped Joanne's with a surprising display of strength. 'I must know the truth, my dear.'

'If Daniel——'

'To the devil with Daniel,' she interrupted forcefully. 'Tell me.'

A warning flashed through Joanne's mind, but, after a brief hesitation, she brushed it aside, and began to explain about Bruce, her need for funds, and Daniel's desire to make his mother happy. It came out haltingly at first, then the sheer relief of being able to tell the truth made the words tumble out in a rush until there was nothing more to say, and she lapsed into a silence that was all at once frightening. What had she done?

'I never thought Daniel could be so foolish,' Serena Grant remarked sadly. 'But I'm so glad he's able to help Bruce. He's such a nice boy.'

'Mother, if Daniel ever finds out that I told you——'

'I shall leave you to tell him one day when you've sorted out your marriage,' she interrupted Joanne understandingly, her blue gaze searching Joanne's with a measure of urgency. 'You do want it to be a real marriage, don't you? You're not just saying so to pacify me?'

'I lie very badly, remember?'

Serena Grant nodded, satisfied. 'Yes, you do, and I know you meant it.'

Joanne leaned forward and brushed her hand lightly over the grey head. 'Mother ... knowing the truth hasn't made you unhappy, has it?'

'No,' she smiled. 'I'm quite satisfied now that I know everything, but I owe you an apology.'

Joanne's hand stilled its stroking movements. 'An apology?'

'Yes, my dear child. If I hadn't been so foolishly eager to see Daniel married, he might have wooed you in his own good time, and then none of this would have been necessary.'

'Oh, Mother ... don't say that,' Joanne whispered, the thought of Daniel ever wooing her too unlikely to contemplate. 'Getting to know you and love you has been an experience I shall always remember with gratitude.'

'You're a sweet child.'

'You're tired,' Joanne replied softly. 'Go to sleep now.'

'Joanne ... give him a little time.'

'I'll give him all the time he wants,' she promised, bending over Serena Grant to kiss her on the forehead. 'Goodnight, Mother.'

During the next few days as Serena Grant's condition grew steadily worse, a new fear replaced Joanne's feeling of relief. She had broken her word to Daniel, and she had no way of knowing how he would react if he should discover this. Would he understand, or would his faith in her be shattered completely?

'You've been very thoughtful lately,' Daniel remarked as he followed her out on to the stoep one evening after dinner. 'Care to talk about it?'

Joanne pushed her hair away from her hot forehead, welcoming the coolness of the night air against her face. 'I've been thinking about your mother—and about us.'

'Your thoughts about Mother I can understand, but what is it about us that troubles you?'

'Oh, just our marriage in general. Nothing specific, really,' she replied vaguely, intensely aware of his tall, dark shape standing so close to her.

'Are you in a hurry to be free, Joanne?'

'You make that sound as though you're asking me whether I'm in a hurry for your mother to die, and you know I'm not, I——'

'Joanne!' he interrupted, turning her roughly to face him. 'Forget my mother for the moment. Are you in a hurry to be free of *me*?'

A pulse leapt oddly in her throat. 'N-not particularly.'

'And what exactly does that mean?' he asked, lowering his head to take a closer look at her in the dull light that filtered through the living-room curtains.

'Well, I'm not going to rush to a lawyer the moment— the moment——' The words choked her. 'Oh, Daniel!'

'Joanne.'

His hand moved across her shoulder, slipped beneath the wide collar of her silk blouse, and came to rest finally against the nape of her neck, his caressing fingers sending a tingling sensation along her nerves.

'Don't ... please!'

'When you tremble like this I want to hold you in my arms,' he said, his breath fanning her forehead. 'Joanne, you're not averse to my kisses, I know that. Do you think that some day you might consider giving our marriage a chance?'

'You mean—make it a real marriage?' she asked in surprise, trying to ignore the sensuality of his touch.

'Why not? Would it be so impossible?'

'But you don't love me,' she protested, clenching her hands at her sides and quelling the desire to touch him.

'Love, Joanne, is a word that's been used too often until it has become meaningless. I think that, given the opportunity, we could make a success of our marriage, and I'm willing to give it a try, if you are.'

'I—I don't know,' she whispered hoarsely. 'I shall have to think about it.'

A smile touched his lips. 'I shan't rush you, my dear. Take your time. But I might as well warn you that I'm no longer going to limit my kisses to when we have an audience. There are other times when I've wanted to kiss you for my own sake, like now for instance.'

Before she could protest, his lips had fastened on to hers, and all desire to resist was swept aside as his arms drew her close against the hardness of his body. She could feel the warmth of his skin through the thinness of his shirt, and her hand lingered for a moment where she could feel his heavy heartbeat. It would be so easy to give him her answer that very minute, but how could she when it would not be a marriage based on love for Daniel?

'No more, please,' she begged eventually, her hands against his chest.

'Then stop trembling.'

'I'm *not* trembling.'

'Liar,' he laughed softly against her throat. 'Joanne, you will consider my suggestion?'

'Yes—yes, I said I would,' she replied, anxious to escape the sensual touch of his hands. 'Daniel, let me go.'

'Must I?'

'Please!'

His hand touched the side of her breast. 'Your heart is beating so fast.'

'Daniel, for pity's sake!' she pleaded when her heart began to race at a suffocating speed.

'All right,' he said, releasing her abruptly, and moving a step away. 'There's no need to panic. I'm not that desperate . . . yet.'

Her cheeks flamed. 'You make me think that all your suggestion boils down to is—sex.'

'What could be more important that that?' he wanted to know, lighting a cigarette and leaning against the low wall, his manner infuriatingly confident.

'Oh!' she exclaimed angrily. 'You're hateful!'

'If you find me so hateful, then why do you tremble each time I touch you?' he demanded, drawing hard on his cigarette.

'It's disgust!' she lied defensively, her agitation increasing when he laughed suddenly.

'No, my Joanne, it's not disgust that makes you tremble, just wholesome desire.'

'Never!' she argued fiercely, wishing she could slap that smug look off his face.

'We shall see.'

His laughter mocked her as she fled inside, but she never reached the sanctuary of her room, for Sister Johnson confronted her in the passage, a worried look on her usually placid face.

'Mrs Grant, you offered your assistance some time ago, and I think I'm going to need it from now on.' She met Joanne's steady glance. 'Mrs Grant senior needs someone in attendance twenty-four hours a day now.'

Shock rippled through Joanne, then her years of training took over, giving her the courage to approach the problem professionally. 'Shall we take it in four-hour shifts as from this very moment?'

'That would be a tremendous relief, Mrs Grant.'

'Make it Joanne, then there won't be any confusion,' she said briskly. 'If you'll just fill me in on the prescribed treatment?'

Sister Johnson nodded and took Joanne through to Serena Grant's room, and for the next few minutes Joanne listened with deep concentration.

'What's all the fuss about?' Serena Grant asked weakly.

'No fuss, Mother,' Joanne assured her calmly. 'From this evening onwards I'm going to give Sister Johnson a break every now and then.'

'Am I getting worse?'

Joanne stared down into those blue eyes dulled with pain, and felt her heart contract violently. 'We're just intensifying the treatment, Mother.' She glanced over her shoulder at Sister Johnson. 'Get some rest while you can, Sister.'

'I haven't much longer, have I, Joanne?' Serena Grant asked once they were alone, and Joanne swallowed violently at the lump in her throat.

'Please, Mother, don't say things like that!'

'My dear, I've known for such—a long time now that —that this day would come,' the words came with diffi-culty, as if a great tiredness had enveloped her. 'I'm not afraid to die, Joanne. It will be a merciful release from this p-pain I've had to endure for so long.'

'Mother——'

'Joanne . . .' she interrupted with her usual determina-tion. 'Would you read to me as you always do? Your voice—so soothing.'

'What shall I read to you, Mother?' she asked, taking the small Bible from the bedside table, and paging through it she prayed silently that her voice would not desert her on this occasion.

'Nothing too sad,' Serena Grant sighed, the injection Sister Johnson had given her taking effect. 'I always liked that thirteenth chapter about love in the first book of Corinthians. Read it to me again.'

Joanne found the place and read to her quietly, but when she reached the end of the seventh verse, Serena Grant gestured that she should read it again.

'Love never gives up; its faith, hope, and patience never fail,' Joanne read to her softly. 'Love is eternal.'

'Love is eternal,' Serena Grant repeated after Joanne.

'Aren't those the most beautiful words, Joanne?'

'Yes, the most beautiful,' Joanne agreed, and Serena Grant closed her eyes and went to sleep.

Two days later, just after midnight, Joanne stood beside Daniel's bed and shook him gently.

'Lorelei,' he murmured in his sleep, drawing her closer.

'Daniel, your mother is asking for you,' she pleaded in an anguished voice, and he was instantly wide awake, leaping out of bed, and pulling on his dark blue dressing gown before Joanne had time to reach the door.

It was the last time Serena Grant spoke to anyone, for, less than an hour later, she went into a coma and, before the sun could rise over Table Bay, she was gone.

'I'm so sorry, Daniel,' said Joanne, catching a trembling lip between her teeth as he turned away from the window, his face haggard, and dark stubbles of beard on his lean jaw. 'It sounds so terribly inadequate at a time like this, but——'

'I know,' he cut in, the roughness in his voice touching her heart as he drew her head down on to his chest. Her arms circled his waist and they clung together for a moment as if to draw strength from each other. His cheek was rough against her own, and then he drew away. 'I'd better go and shave, there'll be plenty to do this morning.'

'If there's anything I could do to help?'

Daniel nodded. 'You could telephone my secretary and ask her to cancel all my appointments for this morning. Then you can telephone the hospital and tell them I shall be doing my rounds a little later than usual this morning.' He passed a tired hand over his eyes. 'The rest I'll see to myself.'

Dr Erasmus came early that morning after Sister Johnson had telephoned him, and shortly afterwards there was nothing except an empty bed where Serena Grant had lain, and an aching emptiness in Joanne's heart.

Sister Johnson remained until after the funeral and, as she carried her suitcases into the hall to await her taxi, she handed a sealed envelope to Joanne.

'Mrs Grant asked me to give you this when it was all over,' she told Joanne. 'She was most explicit about that, and that you had to be alone when I gave it to you.'

Joanne stared at the shaky handwriting on the envelope and blinked back her tears. 'Thank you, Sister Johnson, and thank you for everything you did for Mrs Grant. I'm sure my husband has spoken to you already.'

Sister Johnson nodded, then, as her taxi came crunching up the drive, she held out her hand and clasped Joanne's. 'Goodbye, Joanne, and God bless.'

Joanne stared at the envelope in her hand after Sister Johnson had gone and, going into her room where she could be alone, she slipped her thumb beneath the flap and opened it.

'My dear Joanne,' Serena Grant's spidery handwriting leapt out at her from the page, 'I am writing this while I still find myself capable of holding a pen. Later—who knows but God?

I want you to know that, had I been able to choose, I could not have chosen a more loving and dear wife for my son and, knowing the truth, I am happier than I deserve to be.

I am confident that your love for Daniel will find a way to overcome the obstacles between you, but may I issue a word of warning—don't enter into a real marriage unless there is complete truth between you. It never pays to conceal things from each other. Tell Daniel that I knew the truth before my death, and tell him, too, that my hap-

piness was even greater knowing that my son loved me
enough to go to such lengths to ensure my happiness.

I love you both very dearly, and I know that one day
you will be rewarded for your loving kindness towards
the impossible old woman that I am.' It was signed.
'Serena Grant.'

Joanne, strangled by the tears she could no longer control, fell across her bed and wept until she felt drained
and shaky, and considerably calmer.

CHAPTER SEVEN

THE silence in the house, without Serena Grant and Sister Johnson, was almost too much to bear, and Joanne found the loneliness gnawing away at her. Daniel spent his days at the hospital during those first two weeks after the funeral, and his evenings closeted in his study, shutting Joanne out by his aloofness as surely as if he had turned the key in the lock.

There was no longer any purpose for their marriage to continue, and his suggestion that they consider making it a real marriage was never mentioned again. The opportunity to discuss it never arose, and neither did Daniel give her any encouragement to speak of the things that troubled her. Instead, they shared silent meals, and seldom saw each other in between. It was a most unsatisfactory situation, and Joanne, used to being active, found she was bored to distraction.

The winter rains in the Cape had begun, driving her indoors to escape the chilling dampness, and the bleakness of the grey sky, but, after two weeks of near solitude, she was almost desperate to put an end to her misery. It was Daniel, strangely enough, who made the first move, and Joanne could only imagine that the unsatisfactory situation had troubled him as well when there was a sharp tap on the connecting door one evening while she was brushing her hair before going to bed.

'There's something I want to discuss with you,' he said abruptly, and Joanne nervously fingered the cord of her silk dressing gown as she rose from the stool and faced him.

'There are a few things I want to discuss with you as well, Daniel,' she said, thinking that the darkness of his roll-necked sweater and pants gave his lean body the appearance of a sleek panther with its true strength hidden when the hunting instinct was not there. 'Our marriage, for instance,' she added when he glanced at her strangely.

'Ah, yes—our marriage,' he said with a hint of mockery curving his mouth. 'Are you in a hurry to end it?'

Joanne tugged once more at the cord of her gown and turned away. 'It's not that I'm in a hurry to end it, Daniel, but we must come to some decision about what we're going to do. I can't sit about here indefinitely, doing nothing with my life, and feeling totally redundant.'

'What would you suggest we do?' he asked with a casualness that chilled her.

'I suggest we discuss the possibility of having our marriage annulled some time in the future so I can get myself a job somewhere which would at least give me something with which to occupy my time.'

'Is that me talking?' she wondered when with every part of her being she wished that he would show some sign that he cared.

'You don't, in other words, think we could make our marriage work out?' she heard him ask softly, and her mouth went dry.

'I—Daniel, I——' she faltered helplessly, and stopped.

'I did suggest it once, didn't I?'

'Yes, but—I thought—I didn't think you were really serious.'

'I *am* very serious about it, and I was hoping you would give me your answer.'

'Now?' she asked wide-eyed as she swung round to face him. 'You want an answer now?'

He thrust his hands into his pockets and nodded. 'Why not? You've had enough time to think about it during these past weeks.'

Her heart fluttered to a halt and raced on again.

'Do you—do you think a loveless marriage has any chance of succeeding?'

Daniel's eyes flickered strangely as he came towards her, then, sliding his hand beneath her hair to the nape of her neck, he drew her towards him relentlessly and kissed her long and hard on the mouth until she trembled against him.

'Does that answer your question?'

'A marriage built on a purely physical foundation doesn't sound very secure to me,' she argued shakily, his nearness affecting her pulse rate. 'What happens when I no longer attract you physically?'

'That's the future, Joanne,' he remarked softly, his fingers making persuasive little movements against her neck. 'What we're discussing now is the present.'

'But the present affects the future. A real marriage carries with it certain responsibilities which can't always be ignored.'

'I don't think you'll find me the kind of man who would shirk his responsibilities,' he informed her with the semblance of a smile on his lips. 'Am I?'

'No,' she admitted readily, 'but I wouldn't want a husband who felt honour bound to remain with me.'

'Joanne, let's stop evading the issue. Will you become my wife in the true sense or not?' he demanded, his hand sliding down the centre of her back to draw her closer, but she twisted herself free and put some distance between them.

It was no longer merely a question of saying yes or no to Daniel's suggestion. There was a confession she had to make before she could hope to experience any happiness at all with this man she loved so deeply, and it was a confession she could not delay a minute longer, judging by his impatience. If he still wanted her afterwards then she would accept what he had to offer, and pray that the future would afford her the opportunity to make him care.

'Before I give you my answer, Daniel, there's something I have to tell you,' she began, facing him with a feeling of trepidation.

His glance flicked lazily over her. 'Are you going to tell me you snore in your sleep?'

'Daniel, be serious, please!' she begged.

'Very well, I'm listening,' he laughed mockingly, but Joanne, faced with the moment of truth, found her courage wavering as she sought desperately for some way of breaking the news to him gently. 'Well?' Daniel demanded eventually, his expression indicating that his patience had been tried to the utmost. 'Are you going to tell me or aren't you?'

'Daniel, I——' She broke off abruptly, passing her tongue across her dry lips before she tried again. 'I told your mother the truth before she died.'

One could have heard a pin drop during the ensuing silence as she watched horrified at the change that came over him. His features had become as dark and menacing as his clothes. He was like a panther preparing to pounce, and all at once the spacious master bedroom seemed far too small to accommodate them both.

'You did *what*?' His harsh voice rasped along her already tender nerves.

'I told her the truth,' she whispered, striving for calmness. 'I *had* to. She——'

'You told her the truth about our marriage?'

'Yes, but——'

'You gave me your word you would never tell her, and I trusted you,' he interrupted her with a deadly calm that sent shivers up her spine as he towered over her, his eyes dark and frightening.

'I know I gave you my word, Daniel, but she——'

'You deliberately went against my wishes, and ruined everything in the process,' he cut in once more, not giving her the opportunity to explain the fact that Serena Grant had suspected the truth, nor to show him the letter which would have explained everything so well.

'She wasn't un——'

'I could kill you!' he exploded with a savagery that stripped her of every vestige of colour as he seemed to swoop down on her. She flinched and closed her eyes, thinking he was about to strike her, but the blow never fell. Instead, her shoulders were gripped so cruelly that she feared they would be dislocated as he dragged her against him with a force that choked off the cry that rose to her lips.

'Daniel—please—let me explain,' she gasped frantically.

'Explain?' he roared, his chest heaving beneath her hands as she tried to push him away. 'You've explained enough!'

'Daniel, our marriage,' she pleaded, her eyes filling with tears as the pain shot from her shoulders into her back and arms.

'Our marriage is no longer of any importance to me, but you're not getting away with it that easy.' His grip on her shoulders was mercifully no longer there, but his arms were suddenly latched about her slender body and, for the first time in her life, she knew real fear as she began to suspect his intentions. 'You broke your word to me,' he said through his teeth. 'Now I shall break mine.'

'No! No, don't!' she pleaded, her heart drumming so loudly against her temples that she felt faint as she tried to avoid his mouth. 'Daniel, listen to me. Please!'

'I've listened enough, and it's no use fighting, Joanne, because there's no escape for you. Not this time.'

'You're mad!' she cried as his lips raked her neck and shoulder.

'Yes, I'm mad!' he agreed harshly, his eyes blazing down into hers with such fierce intensity that they seemed to scorch her very soul. 'Mad with rage, and if you were a man I think I would have thrashed you to within an inch of your life!'

His hand tugged sharply at her hair, making her cry out in agony. She pummelled her fists against his chest, but the agony merely increased as he half dragged her towards the bed. His mouth came down on to hers with a force that bruised her lips, and in the struggle the cord of her dressing-gown had come undone, parting at the front to reveal a flimsy nightdress that left very little to the imagination. With a fierce tug Daniel relieved her of her gown seconds before she felt herself fall backwards on to the bed with him pinning her down with his weight.

'Let me go!' she cried, but her cry became a scream of terror as her nightdress was torn from neck to hem. 'Daniel, I beg of you, don't do this!'

'Keep quiet!' he said against her lips, his breathing heavy and laboured. 'The time for talking is over!'

With a last desperate effort she tried to fight him off,

but her strength was puny in comparison to his. The tears ran unheeded down her cheeks as she felt the cruel touch of his hands on her naked body, and the bruising hardness of his mouth as he silenced her pleas for mercy, but there was nothing merciful in that muscular body above her. Daniel had become intent upon taking what he wanted, his anger passionate and unrelenting, and there was no way that she could prevent him from taking what she would have offered gladly had he shown the slightest sign of gentleness.

Joanne awoke the following morning with the sound of someone moving about in the room next to hers. It would be Daniel getting ready to go to the hospital, she realised vaguely, but she was wide awake suddenly as she recalled what had happened the night before. The memory of his brutality was only too vivid, as vivid as the bruises on her arms and body, and so also the bitterness in the angry words she had flung at him moments before he had left her. He had taken his revenge, but it had left him subdued, a brooding expression on his face as he stood beside the bed staring down at her in silence.

'I shall hate and despise you as long as I live,' she had said and, his lips tightly compressed, he had returned to his own room.

She had no doubt that he hated her as much as she now hated him. There was now absolutely no possibility of her ever remaining with him, not after the humiliation she had suffered at his hands. She had always considered him a reasonable man, but he had not so much as given her the opportunity to explain. If he had given her the chance to speak, then this might not have occurred, but he had been caught up in the most terrible anger she had ever seen, and nothing she could have said or done would have made the slightest difference to him.

As she eased her aching body into a hot bath some minutes later, she had already made up her mind about what to do and, centring her thoughts on her future plans, she bathed and dressed warmly before applying a little more make-up than usual to hide the shadows beneath her eyes and the slight puffiness to lips that were still tender to the touch. Now that she had a purpose in mind, she worked swiftly, dragging her suitcases down from the wardrobe and packing a few essential items of clothing. The rest of the expensive wardrobe which Daniel had insisted she buy could remain where it was for all she cared, and there was enough in her personal savings account to keep her for several months until she found suitable employment, preferably out of Cape Town, and somewhere quiet where she would have the opportunity to gather together what was left of her life, to start anew. Perhaps she might be able to look back one day and be thankful for a heart that was whole again, as it had been before Daniel had crushed it so brutally. That part of her life was now in the past, and she intended to keep it there. The future was hers to do with as she pleased, and there was no place for Daniel, or any other man, in what she was planning.

With her suitcases in the hall and the taxi on its way, Joanne went through to Daniel's study and, seating herself behind his desk, she drew his scribbling pad towards her.

'Daniel,' she wrote hastily, 'I'm leaving you, as I can't think you would want me to remain in your home, and neither do I want to stay. I shall be going somewhere where I know I shall be needed, and if there's the slightest shred of decency left in you, then you won't try to find me, or see me again.

You may not believe this, but your mother died happier knowing the truth, but please don't take my word for it.

I shall always be grateful for the way you're helping Bruce. You can at least trust him not to let you down, as you consider I have done. I'm making it easy for you to divorce me, but whether you do or not makes no difference to my future plans.'

She scribbled her name at the bottom and found an envelope in the drawer, but the sparkling yellow diamond on her finger drew her attention. She fingered it lovingly for a moment, then removed both her rings from her finger and dropped them into the envelope before adding a postscript to her letter.

'I'm enclosing the engagement and wedding rings you gave me. They were part of the farce we had planned, and it's a part of my life I want only to forget.'

Folding the letter, she slipped it into the envelope as well, and sealed down the flap before writing Daniel's name on the outside. Then, leaving it on his blotter where he would find it the moment he came in, she hurried out to find her taxi waiting in the driveway.

Less than an hour later she stood looking about her in the rather bare hotel room with its white linen and impersonal atmosphere. Her suitcases stood at the foot of the bed. She had to unpack her things, but first she had to telephone Bruce and let him know where she was, and, going across to the telephone on the bedside table, she lifted the receiver and asked for an outside line. A few seconds later her brother answered the telephone in his flat.

'Bruce,' she began without preamble, 'I'm at the Gateway Hotel close to the municipal gardens.'

There was a momentary silence at the other end before he said impatiently, 'Yes, I know where that is, but what the devil are you doing there?'

'I'll explain, if you could come round and see me as soon as possible.'

'I have a lecture to attend at two this afternoon, so I'll come at once.' Again there was a slight pause. 'Jo ... is Daniel with you?'

Joanne's fingers tightened on the receiver. 'No.'

'There's nothing wrong, is there?' he demanded hesitantly.

'I can't explain on the telephone, Bruce,' she replied, finding her own voice strange to her ears, and so completely lifeless.

'I'll be there as soon as I can.'

Joanne put down the receiver and covered her face with her hands for a moment. It felt as though there was a great emptiness inside her, an emptiness that left her numb and without feeling. She did not want to think of Daniel, not at that moment when all she could see was his face distorted by that terrible anger she had not thought him capable of. She rubbed her arms absently where the sleeves of her dark blue woollen dress hid the bruises left by his cruel fingers, as she made a silent vow that no man would ever have the opportunity to touch her again.

She shivered suddenly and rose to switch on the air-conditioner, turning the dial in order to circulate the warm air through the room while she unpacked her suitcases. She worked steadily for some time before a knock at her door made her push a tired hand through her hair before she went to open it.

'Jo?' Bruce glanced at her anxiously, his hands dug

deep into the pockets of his denims, and the bulky woollen sweater making him look broader in the shoulders than he actually was.

'Come in, Bruce,' she said quietly, a little warmth stealing about her heart at the sight of him. 'I'm sorry the room looks a bit of a mess, but I only arrived a little over an hour ago, and I haven't had time to sort things out yet.'

'Have you left Daniel?' he asked as she closed the door.

'Yes,' she said, turning and gesturing that he should sit down in the only available chair. 'Yes, I have.'

'Why?' he demanded with concern, but Joanne merely shook her head and remained silent. 'For heaven's sake, Jo, there must be a reason!'

Joanne sat down on the bed and lowered her glance to her tightly clenched hands in her lap, finding them strangely bare without her rings. 'My reasons are personal, Bruce, but I'm never going back.'

'Does he know yet that you've left him?'

'He'll know tonight when he arrives home.'

'For God's sake, Jo,' Bruce exploded, pushing an agitated hand through his fair hair. 'He's such a nice guy, and I thought you loved him.'

'I . . . thought so too . . . once,' she admitted reluctantly, a flicker of pain in her glance. 'Bruce . . . if he should ask for my address, promise me you won't give it to him? Please, Bruce?'

'Am I supposed to lie to him and tell him I don't know where you are?' He brought out a squashed packet of cigarettes and lit one with shaky hands. 'Hell, Jo, you know he won't swallow that line.'

'I don't care what you tell him, as long as you don't

tell him where I am.' She leaned forward and placed her
hands on his knees, her glance imploring. 'Bruce, I don't
often ask you to do me a favour. Just this once, give me
your promise?'

'All right, you've got it,' he said after a lengthy silence.
'I'm not going to try and pretend I know what this is
all about, but it's something I never dreamed would
ever happen. You were both so crazy about each other
not even six months ago, and now ...'

'Now it's all over, Bruce, and I intend finding myself
a job somewhere out of the city.'

His eyes widened with dismay. 'You mean you want to
leave Cape Town?'

She nodded slowly. 'I think it would be best.'

Bruce rose to his feet and walked across to the window
where he stood smoking agitatedly for some time before
he turned to face her once more. 'Jo, are you sure you're
not making too much of a little tiff?'

'This wasn't just a little tiff, it——' She broke off
sharply, gesturing angrily with her hands. 'Credit me with
some intelligence, Bruce.'

'I'm sorry,' he said gently, instantly at her side as he
placed an arm about her shoulders and drew her against
him. 'I had to make sure.'

Joanne put her arms about his waist and buried her
face against him. 'We were always very close, Bruce, and
I had to let you in on my plans. I couldn't just disappear
without telling you.'

'I know,' he replied, brushing a hand over her hair.
'And I'm damned sorry things didn't work out between
Daniel and yourself.'

Joanne sighed and stood up, moving across to the
dressing-table where she had placed some of her personal

items until she could find a suitable place for them. She idly fingered her hairbrush, meeting Bruce's glance in the mirror. 'You're very fond of him, aren't you?'

Bruce nodded, his face almost as pale and drawn as her own. 'Yes, I like him very much. He's the kind of guy I always hoped you would marry. Beneath all that abruptness he's a very sensitive man, and a very clever one too. He has made a name for himself as a surgeon, but to meet him, you'd never think so, because he's not conceited.'

That was how she had always thought of Daniel, Joanne realised after Bruce had left. She had thought him the most wonderful man she had ever known and, along with several other nurses, she had placed him on a pedestal, but the pedestal had crumbled violently the night before.

Joanne shuddered. Daniel had had a right to be angry. She had broken her word to him, and no explanation could have altered that. Then Daniel, in turn, broke his, using the most obvious weapon with which to punish her and, lord, how she wished it could have been different. She loved him, and had wanted him, but not like that! Not with such brutal violence that her body still ached from his touch.

There were no tears left to shed. She had shed them all the night before after he had left her in peace, but the rawness in her heart was something she would have to learn to live with, for the healing process would take the rest of her life.

Two weeks later Joanne received a call from Bruce, asking her to meet him at the open-air tea-room in the botanical gardens, and it was there, on that surprisingly warm morning in July while they drank their tea and fed their cake crumbs to the pigeons, that Bruce gave her the news of Daniel's departure.

'He's stored his furniture and put the house up for sale. Daniel received an offer some weeks ago to work at a clinic in Switzerland for a year, and he's now decided to accept it.'

'How—how do you know this?' she asked, a cold hand gripping her heart until it ached numbly.

'Well ...' Bruce avoided her glance, 'I've been seeing him quite often lately.'

'You've been seeing him?' she asked incredulously, watching the embarrassed colour seep beneath his fair skin.

'Yes.' He frowned then, meeting her glance. 'I haven't any quarrel with him, Jo, and ... as he's paying my university fees ...' He moved his shoulders uncomfortably and applied himself to feeding the pigeons as they fluttered their wings and settled on their table.

'Yes, of course,' Joanne said slowly, raising her glance to the majestic Table Mountain as it towered over the city, and wishing her heart could have been carved out of such indestructible rock. 'Did he ... did he say anything about ...'

'About the two of you breaking up?' Bruce finished for her when she faltered to a halt, and she nodded silently. 'Just that your marriage had been a mistake he would regret all his life.'

'Oh,' she said feebly. What had she expected? she wondered as the hand about her heart became a claw with sharp talons. Their marriage had been a mistake; a mistake he would regret all his life. How he must hate her, she decided unhappily. 'When does he leave?'

'He left last night,' Bruce informed her, his words like a douche of cold water in her face.

'I ... see.'

'There's no need for you to leave Cape Town now, is there?' Bruce asked after a lengthy pause as he watched the sunlight glinting on her hair and casting shadows beneath her eyes.

'I'm afraid it's too late. I accepted a post as theatre Sister at a surgical clinic in a place called Willowmead.'

'That's about a hundred and fifty kilometres from here.'

'I know,' she sighed, forcing a smile to her lips, 'but as soon as I'm able, I'll buy a small second-hand car, then I can at least come and see you occasionally when I have time off.'

Bruce accepted this in silence, then, shooing away the pigeons, he leaned towards her across the table. 'Jo ... about Daniel.'

'Please!' Her fingers tightened on her handbag. 'That's an episode that's all over and done with.'

'Not quite,' Bruce insisted stubbornly. 'You still love him, don't you.'

It was a statement, not a query, but with Bruce obviously in such close contact with Daniel, she could not admit the truth.

'I shall always admire him as a surgeon.'

'Is that all?' Bruce asked, and Joanne lowered her lashes to avoid his probing glance.

'That's all I'm prepared to say at this moment.'

CHAPTER EIGHT

JOANNE lowered herself wearily into the chair behind her desk, welcoming the cup of tea her assistant placed before her after the gruelling hours spent in the theatre. Everyone had been unusually tense that morning, from the surgeons down to the junior nurse, and Joanne had found herself in the middle of it all when tempers had become frayed.

'I wonder when Dr Ellis's new partner will arrive,' Alice Fraser voiced the thought which had been the cause of all the trouble. 'There's been such a mystery surrounding this new man that I'm dying to know who he is.'

'According to the grapevine he's already moved into Dr van Amstel's old house, so we should know soon enough,' Joanne replied without particular interest as she studied the theatre list for that day over the rim of her cup and noticed that only one more operation was scheduled for later that afternoon. She glanced at the watch pinned to the front of her spotlessly white uniform, and mentally calculated that she would have enough time to get her log book up to date before returning to the theatre to check that everything was in readiness.

'Aren't you at all curious, Sister Webster?' Alice asked, envying Joanne her slenderness when she herself was so inclined to be on the plump side. 'Dr van Amstel was such an old darling to work for, and the new man might turn out to be a tyrant.'

'A surgeon becomes a tyrant only when the theatre

staff are incompetent,' Joanne replied coolly. 'No one can accuse us of incompetence.'

'Not with you as theatre Sister, they can't.'

Joanne smiled briefly, but her heavily lashed green eyes remained cool. She was aware of the compliment, but aware also of the curiosity in Alice's glance which she had no intention of satisfying.

After a little more than a year as theatre Sister at the Willowmead Clinic, Joanne still remained coldly aloof from the other members of the staff, preferring to spend her free time alone in the flat she had acquired so cheaply, reading, or listening to records, and spending the occasional week-end with Bruce in Cape Town. Men seldom featured in her life, yet she never lacked escorts to the functions she unavoidably had to attend, and the few who unwisely wished for a closer relationship were put firmly in their place. Life was far less complicated without a member of the opposite sex in the background, she believed adamantly.

'Everyone thought Dr van der Merwe would become Dr Ellis's new partner,' Alice remarked. 'Including Dr van der Merwe.'

This much Joanne had deduced from Dr van der Merwe's irritability since it became known that a surgeon was coming out from Europe to take Dr van Amstel's place. As Dr van der Merwe had worked so closely with Dr van Amstel for so many years, it had come as a surprise to everyone to learn that Dr van Amstel, who had died just recently, should have left it to Dr Ellis to sell his shares in the Clinic without giving Dr van der Merwe the opportunity to step into his place.

'Dr van der Merwe will just have to get used to the idea,' Joanne replied casually, drawing the log book closer and picking up her pen, but her thoughts lingered on the subject. Dr Ellis, now in semi-retirement, would naturally choose someone whom he considered capable of taking over from him.

'I wonder if he's young or old.'

Joanne smiled inwardly at Alice's dreamy speculations, recalling her own curiosity when she was a young student nurse, but that was long before ... She severed the thread of her thoughts instantly, and forced herself to concentrate on the information she was penning in the log book.

Some hours later, after another difficult session in the theatre, Joanne slipped the strap of her bag on to her shoulder and drew the folds of her dark blue cape about her. It was August, and it was still cold in the valley this time of year before the advent of spring.

Tall cypress trees cast long shadows across the well-kept lawns in the late afternoon sun, while the benches beneath the shady oak and chestnut trees were deserted by the patients at this hour of the day. The Clinic, a single-storeyed yellow brick building, had been built on the rise of the mountain that formed part of this valley, and Joanne paused for a moment on her way to the parking area to allow her appreciative glance to dwell on the vineyards stretched out before her further down the valley.

The Willowmead Clinic had been established for patients who needed advanced treatment and surgery to their disfigured, badly scarred bodies, and the beautiful gardens surrounding the Clinic, as well as the valley below, where the vines stood acre upon acre changing colour with the seasons, made an ideal place for them to spend time in during the post-operative period.

The breeze lifted Joanne's cape and, shivering, she

drew it more firmly about her as she made her way hastily towards the small blue Austin parked in the staff parking area. It was a ten-minute drive down to Willowmead itself, and she was in a hurry. She had the week-end off, as well as the Monday, and she intended spending it at a small holiday resort about thirty kilometres further north where she could take a horse and go riding along the mountain pass, or bask lazily in the sun if she chose to.

The engine sprang to life at the first touch of the starter, and a few seconds later she was driving as swiftly as she could along the winding road down to the village where the shops would be closing for the night, and the only activity after dark would be at the local cinema and hotel.

Joanne turned off the main street, and a few blocks further she parked her car in front of an old but well-preserved building which had been altered and transformed into four spacious flats. Hurrying up the steps to the first floor, she unlocked her door and went inside, closing it again quickly to shut out the cold.

It was a more spacious flat than the one she had had in Cape Town, and this time she had not stinted herself with the furnishings. The green velvet of the curtains matched the coverings of the small but comfortable sofa and chairs, and the pale gold carpet was soft beneath her feet as she kicked off her shoes to walk on stockinged feet to her room. Dropping her cape and bag on to her bed beside the ready packed suitcase, she turned to face herself in the mirror.

The starched white cap still perched on her head and, raising her hands, she removed it, at the same time extracting the pins from her hair to let it tumble down to her shoulders, healthy and as soft and shiny as silk without the confining pins as she pushed her fingers through it. The face that stared back at her was subtly different now than from the one seen by her colleagues. Golden-brown hair framed her face, softening the lines of her prominent cheekbones with the hollows beneath, and accentuating the vulnerable curve of her perfectly shaped lips. The eyes, too, were unmasked; no longer coldly aloof, but with a definite hint of suffering in their depths.

'You have a whole week-end ahead of just being yourself,' she told her image with a slight smile. 'And it's going to be heaven!'

After a quick bath she packed the few remaining items she wished to take with her, and a little over an hour after arriving at her flat she was speeding on her way to the fulfilment of the relaxing week-end she had planned for herself. Her week-ends away from Willowmead had become a form of escape; an escape from the woman she had become in her desire to avoid involvements of any nature. Friendships usually led to the exchanging of confidences, and this she was not prepared to do. Her life before she came to Willowmead was private, and concerned no one except herself and ... yes, Daniel. She had awakened many nights with his name on her lips, only to cry herself to sleep again, but that, too, was in the past. She was beginning to forget, she told herself as the lights of her car penetrated the darkness ahead, but she had to clamp down on that little voice inside that reminded her so cruelly of the times her heart had nearly ceased its regular beat at the sight of someone tall, lean and dark.

'Daniel,' she whispered his name. How futile the efforts of the mind when the heart was so totally enslaved. Where was he? she wondered. Could he still be in Europe, or had he returned to Cape Town? His name was seldom mentioned between Bruce and herself, but she knew that Bruce had kept up a correspondence with him since his departure, and it was only with the utmost difficulty that she had refrained from asking for news of Daniel. Bruce never proffered any information either, and her hungry heart had remained unsatisfied.

'Oh, stop it!' she told herself fiercely as she turned off the main road and headed towards the mountains. 'Stop dwelling on a subject that should remain dead and buried in the past.'

Joanne walked into her office on the Tuesday morning and hung her cape and bag on the peg against the wall. The lazy week-end had left her feeling slightly lethargic, but work would soon remedy that, she realised as she glanced at the watch pinned to her uniform. Seven-fifteen. She was a little early, but it would give her the opportunity to look through the list of operations scheduled for the day before Alice reported for duty.

'Good morning, Sister Webster.'

That voice! It *couldn't* be, she thought wildly as she swung round to face its owner and, for a few earth-shattering seconds, it felt as though the walls were about to cave in on her before she froze, her years of training coming to her rescue as she found herself staring up into a pair of cold, piercing blue eyes that were as achingly familiar as the tall, lean frame wearing the long white hospital coat. *Daniel Grant*—the one man who had it in his power to ruin her career and jeopardise her carefully built future at Willowmead if he chose to do so. She had hoped never to see him again, but by some cruel twist of fate he was here at the Clinic, and obviously a member of the staff, judging by his appearance.

The time which had elapsed since their last meeting seemed to fall away as if it had never existed, and she saw again his face, dark with passionate anger, and felt again the touch of his hands, cruel and intent upon punishing.

'I would like to see the list of scheduled operations,' he was saying, his voice dragging her back to the present, and, except for the barely noticeable tremor of her hand as she gave him the list, there was nothing to reveal the frightening thoughts which raced through her mind in that terrifying moment of coming face to face with her past. But, to her intense relief, his glance was impersonal, as if he, too, wished to forget what had once occurred.

'What are you doing here?' she managed after what seemed an eternity.

He glanced up from his scrutiny of the list, his glance berating as it flicked over her. 'I work here.'

'That's obvious,' she remarked with touch of sarcasm, 'but why here?'

'Why *not* here?' His lips twisted into a semblance of a smile that she recalled so well. 'This is where my kind of surgery is done, and it seemed an obvious choice.'

'There are other places,' she argued in a lowered voice, angered by the treacherous behaviour of her heart.

'Oh, I don't know,' he said with lazy insolence. 'I liked the sound of the Willowmead Clinic, and what I've seen of the surrounding countryside appeals to me. I think I could settle here quite comfortably.'

Joanne caught her breath sharply. 'Are you—have you taken over from Dr van Amstel?'

'Yes, I have ... Sister Webster,' he added her name derisively.

Footsteps outside the door forced them to discontinue their conversation, and Alice Fraser walked in, her cheer-

ful face brightening even further as she noticed Joanne's
companion.

'Good morning, Dr Grant. Have you and Sister Webster introduced yourselves?'

'We have,' Daniel said abruptly, returning the list to
Joanne who stood tense and erect as she waited for the
blow to fall, but it did not. Daniel afforded Alice one of
his brief, all-embracing smiles before inclining his head
with polite indifference in Joanne's direction, and striding
from her office.

'Isn't he the most gorgeous man you've ever seen,
Sister Webster?' Alice wanted to know as she subsided
into a chair and clasped her hands to her breast. 'When he
looks at me with those blue eyes of his, my knees turn to
water and I'm ready to swoon at his feet!'

Joanne's eyebrows rose, indicating her irritation. 'You'd
better pull yourself together, Alice. We can't have you
passing out in the theatre each time Dr Grant looks your
way.'

'Don't men interest you at all?' Alice asked incredulously. 'I mean, take Dr Grant. He's the best-looking man
ever to cross the threshold of this Clinic. Doesn't the sight
of him make your heart flutter just the teeniest bit?'

'I can't say that I've noticed,' Joanne said coldly, deny-
ing her heart the opportunity to speak for itself. 'Let's
get to work. The first operation is scheduled for eight
o'clock.'

'Work!' said Alice with mock disgust as she rose to
her feet. 'That's all you ever think of.'

'That's all that's of importance at the moment,' Joanne
smiled briefly. 'Come on.'

Joanne spent the rest of the day feeling as though she
was walking through a minefield. Just one word from

Daniel was all that was needed to send the world rocking beneath her feet. There was no earthly reason for him *not* to speak, and several ethical reasons why he *should*, but he chose to remain silent, and it was this very silence that she found so unnerving.

Fortunately she had only to work with him once that morning, but it was a three-hour operation. In his green theatre gown, cap and mask, he could have been anyone, she told herself in an effort to calm her nerves, but as she watched those skilful hands repairing the badly damaged skin tissue of the patient on the table, she became as fascinated as she had always been in the past. The other surgeons were excellent at their jobs, but Daniel reminded her of an artist at work, displaying delicacy and care in his effort to create a masterpiece.

He had her deepest admiration; he would always have *that*. But nothing more! Not ever again!

It was with a sigh of relief that Joanne allowed the theatre door to swing shut behind her just after five that afternoon, but she felt inexplicably tense when she arrived at her flat some time later. She looked about her a little sadly, realizing that, under the circumstances, she would have to leave. She could not endure another day such as the one she had just gone through.

Shortly after seven that evening when her doorbell rang shrilly, she found it no surprise at all to see Daniel standing on her doorstep.

'Come in. I've been expecting you.'

'Have you?' he asked with mild surprise as he stepped past her into the lounge. 'Do you also know why I'm here?'

'I can guess,' she replied stiffly, 'but I think I can save you the trouble by just giving you this.'

He stared at the envelope in her extended hand, his eyebrows raised enquiringly. 'What is it?'

'My resignation.' He accepted the envelope from her as his glance slid derisively down the length of her, taking in her slacks and warm woollen sweater. 'Why?'

'I can't continue working at the Clinic.' She gestured expressively with her hands. 'Not now.'

A sardonic expression flashed across his face. 'What you are actually saying is that you don't want to work with me. Is that it?'

'Yes,' she replied, clasping her hands behind her back.

'I'm afraid, Sister ... Webster,' he smiled cynically as he lowered himself into a chair and stared up at her with his eyes narrowed, 'I'm not going to accept your resignation.' He paused reflectively. 'Either you continue working as theatre Sister at the Clinic, or I make it known that you're actually Mrs Daniel Grant.'

Joanne drew her breath in sharply, her glance lingering on the short dark hair brushed back so severely from his broad forehead, the aristocratic nose, the stern mouth with the sensuous lower lip, and the firm, arrogant chin. He had not changed much, she decided, except for the faint suggestion of crows' feet beneath eyes that held no laughter at that moment.

'You wouldn't do that, would you, Daniel?'

'Wouldn't I?'

'But that's blackmail!' she cried in disbelief as she remained standing.

Daniel stretched out his long legs and studied the tips of his expensive leather shoes. 'Call it what you like, but the choice is yours.'

'You know very well that I have no choice at all,' she argued, clenching her hands at her sides. 'If it should be discovered that—that I'm your wife, my career will be ruined, and you know it.'

'Not only that, Joanne,' he said with infuriating calmness. 'If I make it known that we're legally husband and wife, then I shall insist that you come and live with me as such.'

'Never!' The word escaped her lips with a violence that surprised even herself.

'As I said—the choice is yours,' he repeated, dropping the envelope which contained her resignation on to the small table between them, and Joanne felt her slender body tremble with anger.

'I hate you!'

'Yes, I know,' he replied carelessly, glancing about him. 'Hm ... nice little place you have here. You have good taste, Joanne. Perhaps you could help with the decor of some of the rooms up at my house.'

Ignoring this, she asked: 'Did you know I was here at Willowmead when you decided to come here?'

His blue gaze met hers with a touch of insolence. 'Yes, I did.'

'Bruce,' she said with conviction, knowing without being told who had offered the information.

'I'm sure he didn't intend to give away your whereabouts, but he's a very honest young man at heart, and I doubt whether he even realises that he mentioned it.' He held her glance compellingly. 'Why didn't you start divorce proceedings when you had the opportunity, Joanne?'

She shrugged and walked away from him, hugging her arms about herself as if they offered some protection. 'I was too busy trying to forget, besides, I thought you ...'

'I was too busy trying to remember,' he said a brief

smile on his lips as she swung round to face him. 'The Swiss Alps is a great place for remembering things one would rather forget. The warm sunshine of one's own country, the sea on a moonlit night, and,' his glance went to her hair, 'the flash of gold in a certain woman's hair.'

'Don't!' she said hoarsely, finding that his lean muscular body, reclining so comfortably in one of her chairs, still had the power to radiate that magnetism she had found so difficult to resist.

'You know, Joanne,' he continued quietly, 'when you're in a strange country you have plenty of time to think. You think about the good things that have happened in your life, and the bad. The sensible, and the foolish. You can't alter what's happened, but you can have a damn good try at not making the same mistakes again.'

Her eyes darkened with suspicion. 'I don't think I quite understand what you're getting at.'

'Don't you?' His lips twitched slightly. 'Perhaps I don't understand it myself. However, here I am at Willowmead, I've bought that lovely old house Dr van Amstel used to live in, and I think I intend to stay.'

Joanne's chin lifted with defiance and determination. 'I'm going to see a lawyer tomorrow.'

'No, you won't,' he said harshly, 'because I shan't give you a divorce.'

'You can't refuse. You could be——'

'I shall install you in my home, by force if necessary, and your claims will be worthless.'

'You think you're very clever, don't you?' she hissed at him, her angry heartbeats pounding against her temples.

'Not really,' he smiled lazily. 'I've acquired a taste for playing games. At first we were married, but pretending that our platonic marriage was real. Now we're married, pretending that we're not.' Again he smiled infuriatingly. 'It's a little confusing, but it would make interesting listening, don't you think?'

His arrogance astounded her. 'I never realised you could be so hateful!'

'I never realised before how beautiful you are when you're angry,' he quipped back, his keen glance flicking over her flushed cheeks, and the way the greenness of her eyes deepened.

'Oh, for goodness' sake!' she exclaimed. 'If you've said all you intended to say, then please go!'

'Don't you usually offer your guests something to drink?'

'You're not a guest,' she retorted angrily, realising her error too late.

'No, I'm your husband,' he said darkly. 'Be thankful that all I'm asking for is a cup of coffee.'

Her cheeks flamed. 'You have a nerve! I——'

'Make that coffee, and be quick about it, or I might change my mind,' he threatened and, hesitating only briefly, she fled to the kitchen and switched on the kettle.

If this was the only way she could get rid of him, then she had no intention of wasting any time about giving him what he had asked for, she thought furiously. Confound the man!

She joined him in the lounge again a few minutes later and placed a cup of coffee on the small table beside his chair. 'I hope it chokes you.'

'Sit down.'

'I——'

'Sit down!' he ordered, gripping her wrist with firm fingers and forcing her into the chair beside his. 'That's better. I've heard quite a lot about you during the few days I've been at the Clinic.'

'Have you?' she asked, her skin still tingling where his fingers had touched her wrist.

'None of it sounds quite like you, though,' he remarked, drinking his coffee quite calmly as if he were in no hurry to leave.

'Really?' she murmured sarcastically.

'Hm ...' he nodded. 'Things such as "cool, aloof and mysterious". It makes me wonder whether I ever knew the real Joanne.'

'What a pity that I shan't give you the opportunity of getting to know me now either.'

'Sarcasm?' he mocked, shaking his head. 'That's not like you at all.'

'I wish you'd go,' she said coldly, staring down at her clenched fists in her lap.

'Inhospitable too, I see,' he laughed briefly, draining his cup and placing it on the table beside him before he pinned her to her chair with those incredibly blue eyes of his.

'Daniel, I've been happy here. Don't make it impossible for me to stay,' she begged now. 'Could we, in future, keep our meetings restricted to the Clinic?'

'That would be rather difficult,' he remarked after a momentary pause, his glance openly mocking. 'I happen to like your company, even when you're so unsociable.'

'I don't happen to like *your* company,' she blurted out angrily, jumping to her feet and wishing at that moment she could throw something at him.

'A pity,' he murmured, following it up swiftly with an abrupt, 'but you'll like my company in time.'

Her temples throbbed. 'Don't be too sure of that.'

To her relief, he rose to his feet, but her pulse jumped

violently as he closed the gap between them, his nearness disturbing her more than she cared to admit.

'Goodnight, Joanne ...' he hesitated mockingly, '... or should I say, Sister Webster.'

Choosing to ignore him, she led the way to the door and opened it. 'Goodnight, Dr Grant.'

She heard his footsteps on the stairs, and moments later a car started down below in the street. Joanne expelled the air from her lungs, realising for the first time that she had been holding her breath for seemingly endless seconds, and then she began to shake quite uncontrollably. How long would she be able to fight against the feelings he aroused within her, and what did he hope to gain by forcing his attentions upon her?

CHAPTER NINE

WHILE having lunch in the canteen the following day, Joanne spotted Dr Chris van der Merwe making his way towards her table. He was of average height, with broad shoulders, rugged features, and brown hair that tended to tumble in an unruly fashion across his forehead. He had accompanied Joanne on two occasions to functions which had been organised by the staff of the Clinic, but she had discouraged a third invitation to attend a dance at the local hotel with him. He was the kind of man who could very easily become serious about the woman he was taking out, and she had no intention of encouraging anyone into an affair; not after what she had been through with Daniel.

'May I join you, Sister Webster?'

His voice was pleasant with a slight Afrikaans accent, and she smiled absently. 'You may.'

'I should like to apologise for my filthy temper these past weeks,' he said, seating himself opposite her and leaning his arms on the table.

'You don't have to apologise to me, Dr van der Merwe.'

'You're right, of course,' he nodded ruefully. 'I should actually be apologising to the entire theatre staff, but I thought that if I explained my behaviour to you, you would at least understand.'

'You don't really have to explain, Doctor,' she said quickly, feeling sorry for him.

'It would make me feel better,' he insisted gravely. 'You see, I'd worked with Dr van Amstel for almost eight years. I knew his techniques so well that when he fell ill and died I thought Dr Ellis would consider me as his next partner. Instead, he sold Dr van Amstel's shares to Dr Grant, a man who has brushed aside Dr van Amstel's ideas in favour of new, modern techniques that make me shudder when I think I have to make use of methods that are unheard of in this country.'

Joanne felt a twinge of pity for him, but her admiration for the work Daniel performed made her jump to his defence. 'Dr Grant is a brilliant surgeon.'

'Oh, yes, I know he has a reputation for accomplishing the impossible,' Chris van der Merwe admitted readily, 'but I had hoped that Dr Ellis would have taken my years of service into consideration.'

'The choice was entirely, Dr Ellis's, I presume?' she asked quietly.

'Definitely! After Dr van Amstel's death his shares went straight back to his partner to do with as he pleased,' he told her. 'It's taken me some time to accept the fact that I wasn't good enough.'

Joanne frowned as she met his glance. 'Don't labour under an inferiority complex, Dr van der Merwe. You're an excellent surgeon, and I've worked with several in my time.'

'You're certainly good for my ego, Sister Webster,' he smiled, and the conversation drifted on to lighter topics until Joanne became aware that someone was watching her closely.

She sent a casual glance across the crowded canteen until it collided with Daniel's thunderous eyes, and her heart thudded uncomfortably as he moved away from the self-service counter, bringing his cup of coffee across to her table.

'Good afternoon, Dr van der Merwe,' he greeted his colleague with cool amiability before his mocking glance met hers. 'Hello, Joanne. I'm sorry I kept you waiting.'

'Take my chair, Dr Grant,' Chris van der Merwe said quickly, rising to his feet after overcoming his initial surprise. 'I was just leaving.'

'What do you mean by barging in on my conversation with Dr van der Merwe, and calmly apologising for keeping me waiting?' Joanne demanded in a lowered voice once they were alone. 'I never arranged to meet you here.'

'No, of course you didn't,' Daniel replied calmly as he took the chair Dr van der Merwe had vacated and stirred his coffee. 'But the two of you looked very chummy from where I was standing, and I wouldn't like the poor chap to get any ideas about you.' He leaned towards her menacingly. 'You're *mine*, and I intend to keep it that way.'

'How dare you!'

'Careful, darling,' he warned softly. 'People are watching.'

'Don't call me "darling",' she said fiercely, lowering her voice more and getting a grip on herself. 'I'm not your darling, and I never shall be.'

His eyes flickered mockingly as he lowered his cup and took in the starched primness of her appearance. 'Never is a long time, Joanne, and my patience is wearing thin.'

'You have no right to lay any claim on me, and what I do outside this Clinic, or in my lunch hour, is *my* business. You had no right to interrupt Dr van der Merwe and myself in that way, giving the impression that—that——'

'That I've taken a fancy to you?' he finished for her

with that infuriating calmness she had noticed the night before, 'Yes, that was exactly the impression I wanted him, and everyone else, to have. I have a certain document locked away at home that says I have every right to be possessive, and I *am* possessive, Joanne. What I have, I hold.'

Her pulse rate became nervous and erratic. 'Why?'

'Why do I want to hold on to you?' Those penetrating eyes beneath the dark brows sent a shiver of apprehension along her spine. 'I happen to like beautiful things, and you're beautiful, my Lorelei.'

'Don't call me that!' she ordered sharply, pain stabbing her heart at the half-forgotten name.

'I would suggest you keep your voice lowered, unless you want everyone in the canteen to sit up and take notice,' he warned mockingly.

'You're despicable!' she hissed.

'Yes, and plenty more besides,' he admitted, draining his cup and following her out of the building into the sunshine. 'I'll see you this evening.'

'I shan't be home,' she announced firmly, quickening her pace, but his fingers latched on to her wrist and forced her to keep in step with him.

'You'd better be,' he threatened, his eyes narrowed against the brilliance of the sun that gave his hair a bluish tint. 'If you're not, all hell will be let loose in the village until I find you.'

When they met again later that afternoon in the theatre, he was his usual abrupt self, giving no indication that he was even aware of the threat he had uttered to her as they had left the canteen, but that evening, as she glimpsed his dark green Citroën from her window, she experienced a wave of helplessness that drove her to anger. Why would he not leave her alone?

The doorbell chimed, and knowing quite well who it was, she called: 'Who is it?'

'Daniel,' his voice came strongly through the door. 'Open up.'

'Go away! I don't want to see you.'

'Joanne ...' There was something ominous in the sound of her name on his lips, and she shivered even before he continued to speak. 'Either you open up this door, or I cause a performance here on your doorstep which should interest your neighbours intensely.'

She hardly knew her neighbours, but the thought of them rushing to their doors to investigate any sort of noise coming from her flat was just too much, and she sighed as she lifted the latch and opened the door wide.

'Come in, then.'

'That's better,' he remarked calmly, kicking the door shut and facing her in the small entrance hall. 'Lorelei, you're as pale as a ghost.'

His arms closed about her with an unexpected force that gave her no time to resist, or to escape the lips that captured hers with a gentleness that shook the barriers she had erected about her heart. His hand was in her hair, scattering the pins on to the floor as he pushed his fingers through the thick silky tendrils.

He released her just as suddenly as he had taken her, and she fell back against the wall, her breath coming fast over parted lips as she stared down at the pins lying at her feet.

'I wish you'd leave me alone!'

'I can't do that, Joanne, and leave your hair down.' His glance slid down the length of her, scorching her through the long-sleeved jersey dress that accentuated her slenderness. 'It makes you look so very feminine, my sea-nymph.'

'Don't call me that!' she flared, her cheeks hot with embarrassment.

'Ah, yes, I forgot,' he smiled cynically. 'Get your coat, we're going out.'

'Out?'

'Yes,' he said abruptly, ushering her towards her room. 'I'm taking you to my home. I need suggestions on how to furnish it.'

'I'm not interested in helping you furnish your home,' she told him firmly, drawing back.

'I shan't buy a single item of furniture for those vacant rooms unless you choose them.'

'For all I care you can live in a partially unfurnished house for the rest of your life,' she spat out angrily.

'Tch, tch,' he shook his head mockingly. 'Such venom dripping from such beautiful lips!'

A tremor of anger shook through her. 'Just leave me alone, Daniel . . . please!'

His eyes darkened. 'I shall shout the place down if you don't come with me.'

'Then shout if you want to.' He opened his mouth as if to do so and she gestured anxiously. 'No, don't!'

'I knew you'd see reason,' he remarked with a satisfaction that made her want to slap his face. 'Get your coat, it's cold outside.'

She was in such a fury that she grabbed the first thing she could lay her hands on, and it was only afterwards that she realised she had taken a camel-hair coat which had been given to her by his mother. She fingered the wide collar, lifting it to lie against her cheek as they sped towards his home. It was strange how close she felt to

Serena Grant at times; close enough to awaken a deep longing within her to hold those thin hands between her own in an effort to seek reassurance.

The car slowed down and she snapped out of her reverie to see the two stone pillars caught in the beam of the lights, then they drove through them and up the long drive towards the double-storeyed house with its thatched roof, its walls covered in ivy creeper, and its wonderful terraced garden leading down to the tennis court and swimming pool.

'After you, my dear,' said Daniel as he unlocked the front door and stood aside. She stepped across the threshold hesitantly, noticing familiar objects in the hall, and wishing herself miles away from the painful memories that seemed to crowd her mind. A hand gripped her arm and steered her off to the right. 'Through here.'

She found herself in the large living-room, but the furniture he had kept from his old home seemed lost in the vastness of the room. 'You've kept most of your furniture, I notice,' she remarked for want of anything better to say.

'Yes, but this is a much larger house. There are eight bedrooms, and only five of them are furnished. The living-room furniture is inadequate, as you can see, but it could go into the family-room quite comfortably. That would mean refurnishing this room, and that's where you come in.' He opened the doors of the large cabinet beside the stone fireplace and took out a bottle and two glasses. 'I think you'd better have a little sherry first to calm you down before I take you on a guided tour of the house.'

'I don't want any sherry.'

'Must you always argue? It's so tiresome.'

'I didn't want to come here with you,' she reminded him.

'But you're here now, so behave like the lady you are and accept my hospitality.' He placed two glasses of sherry on the small circular table beside the fire which burned so lustily in the grate, and came towards her. Forcing herself to remain perfectly still as he helped her off with her coat, Joanne was nevertheless aware of the fact that he was dangerously attractive in his grey tweed jacket and open-necked white shirt that exposed the strong, tanned column of his throat. He drew her towards the chair beside the fire, and pressed a glass into her hand. 'Drink that down. It's guaranteed to smooth your ruffled feathers.'

The liquid scorched her throat, but moments later she experienced a tingling warmth which was not entirely due to the log fire which had obviously been lit shortly before their arrival.

The tour of Daniel's home did not take very long, for she had been there once before when Dr van Amstel had still been alive and, despite herself, she felt a certain eagerness rising within her to fill those lovely rooms with colourful furnishings which would complement the rest of the house.

'I have a catalogue here from which you could make your selection,' Daniel said as they returned to the living-room, 'and it includes samples of curtaining.'

He dropped the thick catalogue into her lap once they had resumed their seats beside the fire, and she stared at it as if it was something obnoxious. 'Daniel, I don't——'

'Please, Lorelei.'

His glance was intense and persuasive, and she found

her resolve crumbling. 'You may not—not like my choice.'

'I know you'll choose well,' he said, sustaining her glance without difficulty, then, as she sighed and began to page through the catalogue, he leaned back in his chair and lit a cigarette, blowing the smoke through his nostrils. 'That's my girl.'

It took longer to select the required items than it took to walk through the entire house, but she was eventually satisfied with her choice as she returned the catalogue with the different items marked clearly with the pen he had handed to her.

'Thank you, Joanne,' he smiled briefly, turning towards the cabinet. 'This calls for another sherry.'

'Not for me, thank you,' she said quickly, only just surfacing from the light-headedness of the first.

'Most definitely for you,' he ordered. 'I can't drink alone.'

'It's late,' she tried again.

'It's barely past nine,' he smiled lazily after a glance at the clock on the mantelshelf, and Joanne somehow found herself with a glass between her fingers, sipping the amber liquid slowly and hoping it would steady the nerve that quivered so incessantly at the pit of her stomach.

'I must go home now,' she said at last, hoping her voice sounded steadier than it felt.

Daniel gestured towards the empty space beside him on the sofa. 'Come and sit here.'

'No!' She recoiled from the suggestion as if a snake had bitten her.

'Afraid?' he mocked, stretching his legs out before him.

'I'm not afraid, but——'

'Then come and sit here beside me. You're not nervous of being alone here with me, are you?'

'No, of course not!' she argued, finally joining him on the sofa to prove her point.

'Relax,' he murmured, sliding an arm along the back of the sofa and caressing the side of her neck with his fingertips. 'I shan't bite you.'

'I've never thought of you as a wolf, Daniel,' she said, shutting her mind to the sensations created by his touch.

'That pleases me very much, Lorelei,' he mocked gently, his breath against her cheek as he slipped his fingers beneath her collar and across her shoulder.

'Don't ... please,' she choked out the words as her nerves quivered responsively to his touch.

He leaned towards her then, forcing her into the curved end of the sofa. His breath was warm against her mouth as he murmured, 'Stop fighting the inevitable, my Joanne.'

'I'm not *your* Joanne.'

'Oh, but you *are*,' he insisted before the warm pressure of his mouth on hers sent her senses reeling helplessly.

She had to fight against the emotions which threatened to overwhelm her, emotions she had thought never to experience again, and she struggled against him, twisting her mouth away from his.

'Let me go! I hate you!'

'I know,' he said, his eyes darkened by passion. 'You hate me just as I hate you, but that doesn't diminish the fact that I find you very desirable.'

Her hands encountered the hardness of his shoulders as she tried to push him away. 'Daniel, stop it!'

'I want you, Joanne,' he whispered hoarsely against

her throat. 'Just as much as you want me at this moment, and don't deny it.'

She knew she had to escape his lips or be submerged in emotions she would not be able to control, but she felt a sharp tug at her hair, forcing her to keep her head still. His kiss was a white-hot passion that seared through her, making a mockery of the defences she had built up over the past year, and stripping her of the desire to resist the uncontrollable force of her emotions. His fingers found the zip at the front of her dress and tugged, then his hand was against her waist, moving across to her back and up along her spine, leaving a trail of fire against her skin as he caressed her, arousing her emotions as one would kindle a fire. He fumbled with the catch of her bra, but as she struggled feebly against him, it gave way and his hand moved round to the front to cup her breast.

She trembled violently, wanting his touch, yet knowing that she dared not allow it, but her body ignored the frantic messages her brain was flashing out as she slipped her arms about Daniel's neck and pressed closer to him.

'Lorelei ...' he muttered against her lips. 'Stay with me. Stay with me tonight.'

'No! I can't!' she cried hoarsely, her mind rejecting his suggestion, while her treacherous body yearned for fulfilment.

'You can,' he insisted, his body hard against her own. 'You're my *wife*.'

'No!' Scraping together every ounce of strength she had left, she twisted away from him and jumped to her feet, pulling up the zip of her dress at the same time. Daniel rose more slowly, coming up behind her, but as he reached out for her she moved away jerkily, her breath coming fast. 'Don't touch me!'

'Stop panicking,' he ordered harshly, not touching her. 'If you stay, then you stay of your own free will. I shan't force you.'

'Take me home, please.'

'This is your rightful home,' he insisted mockingly, but Joanne had had enough. Grabbing her coat, she made a dash for the door, but Daniel was there before her. 'Where do you think you're going?'

Her eyes blazed into his with renewed anger. 'If you won't take me home, then I'll have to walk.'

'I feel like shaking you,' he said through his teeth, taking her coat from her nerveless fingers and holding it for her to slip her arms into the sleeves, then, taking a firm grip on her arm, he said: 'Come on, Sister Webster. I'll take you home.'

The short journey back to her flat was one she knew she would always remember. She sat silently beside him, trying to ignore the discomfort of her loosened bra, and wishing frantically that her heartbeats would subside, but it was a futile wish when her body still tingled with his remembered touch.

When he walked with her up the flight of steps to her flat a few minutes later, she was aware of his brooding stillness beside her. It should have been a warning to her, but it was not and, in the shadows of her doorway, he swept her into his arms and kissed her long and hard. It was a shattering kiss that left her shaken to the core when she eventually made her way inside and locked the door behind her. She heard his car drive away, but she knew too that he took her heart with him. She had fought relentlessly against all impossible odds, but she was now forced to admit defeat. She loved Daniel; loved him despite everything. And Daniel? She sighed inwardly. It was difficult to know just what Daniel was thinking, or if he had a heart at all. He had wanted her to stay with him, but it had been merely to satisfy his physical desire for her. Love never entered into it as far as he was concerned, and it was with this thought that she finally went to sleep that night.

Dr Chris van der Merwe walked into Joanne's office first thing the next morning, and her cool glance detected a certain discomfiture in his attitude towards her as they bade each other good morning.

'That ... er ... conversation we had yesterday,' he began, thrusting his hands into the pockets of his white coat and staring at the floor.

'That conversation was strictly between us, doctor,' Joanne assured him, realising instantly the reason for his strange behaviour.

'Thank you,' he replied, a look of relief flashing across his rugged face. 'I wouldn't want Dr Grant to think I begrudged him his position.'

'Of course not,' she smiled briefly. 'You were disappointed, that's all.'

'You're very understanding, Sister Webster,' he smiled back at her. 'It gave me a bit of a jolt when I heard him being so familiar with you, and calling you Joanne, whereas I ...' His glance became curious. 'Did you know him before he came here to Willowmead?'

'I ...' Joanne hesitated. How much could she tell him without becoming involved in a lengthy explanation? 'Strictly between us, Dr van der Merwe, I *have* worked with him before, but I ...'

'You don't want it known,' he filled in for her as he grasped the situation. 'Did you know him well?'

'Quite well.'

'I see.' His smile became a little twisted. 'I don't suppose I'd stand a chance against him where you're concerned?'

Her heart lurched uncomfortably. 'Doctor, I——'

'Don't answer that,' he interrupted quickly. 'I had no right to be so personal, and thank you for not repeating what I'd told you.'

He raised his hand in greeting and was gone before she could say another word, and she barely had time to sit down behind her desk when Daniel walked in.

'May I see the list for the morning?' he said abruptly as she rose to her feet respectfully and handed him the required list.

While her heart beat out a regular tattoo at his presence, he appeared coldly indifferent and far removed from the man who had held her so passionately the night before. Looking at him now, she found it almost impossible to believe him capable of displaying any emotions whatsoever. His appearance was deceptive, she knew, for beneath that cool, abrupt exterior there lurked a man like any other. She was aware of his sensitivity, had known his gentleness, his virile passion, but most of all she had felt the lash of his violent anger.

'I think I would rather do Mrs Gray's transplants this morning, and Mr Walters' this afternoon,' his deep, gravelly voice dragged her back from her thoughts. 'Would you inform the ward Sisters of the change in the schedule?'

'Certainly, Dr Grant,' she heard herself say in a voice that sounded surprisingly cool, considering the shattering intimacy of the thoughts racing through her mind.

She lifted the receiver to do as he had instructed, feeling curiously deflated when she saw him stride from her office without a backward glance.

When would she learn that she meant nothing to Daniel? she admonished herself silently. Last night, when he had wanted her physically, it had been a different matter, but this morning he was as distant as ever, his glance coldly dispassionate when he had condescended to favour her with it. 'Oh, lord,' she sighed, 'why did I have to fall in love with such a cold slab of a man?'

CHAPTER TEN

DANIEL did not come to her flat that Thursday evening, and, despite herself, Joanne found herself wandering about aimlessly, wishing she could find some excuse to see him, yet knowing that she would never have the audacity to approach him of her own accord.

What was he doing? she wondered. Was he alone in that large house? Alone, and perhaps a little lonely too?'

Pulling herself together sharply, she went through to her room and sorted through the clothes she intended taking with her that week-end. Bruce had telephoned earlier that evening to say that his friend would be away for the week-end, and they could have the flat to themselves if she could make it down to Cape Town the Saturday morning.

'Bring your glad rags with you,' Bruce had instructed. 'We might just go out on the town Saturday night.'

It sounded very unlike Bruce, she thought with a warm smile on her lips, but then he might have reason to celebrate something, and she could not disappoint him.

Joanne kept herself occupied until it was time to go to bed, but she slept badly, her dreams conjuring up images of Daniel and the past which she would rather have forgotten, and she awoke the following morning with a throbbing headache which lingered on during half the day, forcing her eventually to take something stronger than aspirins for relief.

Daniel's abruptness in the theatre was a source of irritation to her as well. Nothing seemed to have affected his night's rest, while she ...! It was not his fault either, she thought charitably. He never asked her to love him. Not once!

That Friday evening, as she packed her suitcase for the week-end, she experienced a tingle of anticipation which was totally alien to her, but when she eventually answered the doorbell to find Daniel on her doorstep, she knew the reason for it.

'I'm rather busy. What did you want?' she demanded rudely.

'Is that the way you welcome visitors?' he mocked, then, as she made no attempt to invite him in, he asked: 'Are you going to leave me standing on the doorstep all night?'

She had wanted him to come, yet now that he was there she shrank from him. 'I suppose you'd better come in.'

'I accept your very ungracious invitation,' he remarked with sarcasm as he brushed past her and entered the lounge.

'Could I make you a cup of coffee? I'm afraid I haven't anything stronger,' she offered after a stab of guilt.

'Coffee will do,' he said abruptly, lowering himself into a chair as she went into the kitchen to switch on the kettle, but she tensed a moment later when she heard his step behind her.

'I noticed the open suitcase on your bed,' he remarked as she swung round to face him. 'Are you going away somewhere?'

'I'm going away for the week-end,' she replied stiffly, aware of his nearness, and that aura of masculinity which always surrounded him.

'Are you going to see Bruce?'

'I ... might see him,' she replied evasively.

Daniel's smile was mocking. 'Why do you sound so cagey?'

'I don't like people prying into my affairs.'

'Neither do I, but when it concerns my wife——'

'I'm not your wife!' Joanne bit out the words, a sparkle of anger in her green eyes.

'You're my wife in every sense of the word, Joanne,' he said with calm deliberation as he approached her. 'I made sure of that before I left for Switzerland. Have you forgotten?'

Joanne swallowed violently and looked away, her body taut with resentment. 'I wish I *could* erase your humiliating cruelty from my memory.'

'I was cruel to you only that once, Joanne,' he said softly, standing so close to her that she could almost feel the warmth radiating from his virile body. 'There were other occasions when——'

'Don't!' she interrupted gratingly, her hands clenched so tightly at her sides that the nails bit into her soft palms. 'I don't want to be reminded of those other occasions.'

'The other night, then,' he persisted ruthlessly.

'No!' she cried, lowering her voice instantly as she gathered her shattered composure about her. 'You—you're rather overwhelming at times, Daniel. You're attractive even if you're abrupt, and already you have the nurses eating out of your hands. Why should I be so—so different from them?'

His glance was rapier-sharp as she challenged him. 'I don't think I want that kind of adulation from you, Joanne.'

'Do you find your pedestal uncomfortable?' she mocked.

To her surprise she saw his firm lips curve into a smile. 'If you were ever foolish enough to place me on it, then I must have taken quite a tumble by now.'

'Yes ...' her lips quivered into a responding smile. 'You did take a tumble when it collapsed beneath you.'

'I'm glad,' he said, his hands on her shoulders sending urgent messages along her receptive nervous system. 'I'm human, Joanne, and I have many faults. Don't ever forget that.'

She lost herself for a moment in the blueness of his eyes until her attention was drawn to the cloud of steam emitting from the electric kettle.

'I'll make that coffee,' she said unsteadily, escaping his touch and putting some distance between them.

'I did some sorting last night, and found something that actually belongs to you,' he remarked casually some time later after they had returned their empty coffee cups to the tray.

'Something that belongs to me?' she queried, her pulse quickening.

'Yes,' he nodded, slipping his hand into his jacket pocket. 'Catch!'

A small velvet-covered box dropped into her lap and, knowing instantly what was inside, she shrank from it inwardly.

'No—no, I can't——'

'Those rings were bought for you, Joanne, and they serve no purpose lying about in my drawer. They belong on your finger,' he continued unperturbed. 'Give me your hand.'

'Daniel ... no,' she choked out the words, but Daniel

crossed the space between their chairs and, gripping her left wrist with his one hand, he opened the small box with the other, lifting the rings from their satin cushions and slipping them on to her finger while she watched in stunned fascination how the stones glittered and sparkled warmly beneath the light.

'That's better,' he said abruptly. 'It's good to have a wife again.'

'I don't want to wear them,' she argued helplessly as he drew her to her feet.

'Do you find it so distasteful to belong to me?' he demanded harshly, and she flinched inwardly.

'I don't belong to you,' she whispered passionately. 'I could never belong to a man like you.'

'One day, Joanne ...' he murmured, breaking the heavily charged silence between them. 'One day I shall lose patience with you, and ...' He muttered something unintelligible, drawing her so forcibly against him that the breath was almost knocked from her body as he kissed her hard and bruisingly on her soft lips. 'Goodnight!'

The front door slammed shut behind him, but Joanne remained where she was, her fingers touching tender lips which could still feel the bruising mastery of his kiss. A flash of light caught her attention and, glancing down at her hand, she wasted no time in tearing the rings from her fingers and replacing them rather roughly in the small box Daniel had dropped on to the table beside her chair. She did not *want* his rings! She did not want to be possessed by such a cold brute of a man!

'Oh, God!' she moaned, sinking sideways into her chair and burying her face in the crook of her arm. 'The trouble is, I *want* to be possessed by him, but more than anything I want to be loved. *Loved*, and not merely *wanted*.'

'How on earth can you live in such a jumbled, untidy atmosphere?' Joanne demanded, her glance sliding over piles of books, files, sheets of paper on which notes had been taken down, university banners hanging from the walls, and left-over rag posters propped up against vases and bookcases. 'Don't the two of you ever spend some time sorting through everything and cleaning up the mess you make?'

Bruce pushed back his chair and using his knee against the side of the table as a lever, he rocked himself gently, a boyish smile spreading over his face. 'We like it the way it is, and don't welcome feminine intervention in our strictly male lair.'

'Then I should feel honoured that my presence has been welcomed, or am I not considered to be feminine?'

Bruce shrugged, his eyes teasing wickedly. 'There are times when one is forced to make allowances for a sister.'

'If you're not careful, I'll throw something at you in a minute,' Joanne laughed, piling the remainder of their supper dishes into the small sink, and opening the tap. 'Are you going to help with the dishes?'

'No,' his arm came round her as he closed the tap. 'And neither is there time for you to do anything. You're going out, remember?'

'*We're* going out,' she corrected, meeting his smiling glance.

'Sure,' he said impatiently, gripping her shoulders and propelling her from the kitchen. 'Now get into that bathroom, and hurry it up, because I need it as well.'

'You know something?' She turned to face him, her

head tilted thoughtfully. 'You're becoming just as arrogantly bossy as ...'

'Yes?' Bruce prompted as her voice trailed off into an embarrassed silence.

'Never mind,' she said abruptly, not wanting to discuss Daniel with Bruce. She was certain somehow that he knew of Daniel's partnership in the Willowmead Clinic, but it was as though they had both meticulously avoided discussing the subject since her arrival that morning.

This was the first time Bruce had actually invited her to stay at the flat he shared with a fellow student, Joanne thought as she soaked in the scented water for a moment before soaping her body. Usually she stayed at a hotel close by, but on this occasion Bruce had insisted that, with his friend away for the week-end, she would be welcome to rough it with him.

Roughing was the operative word, she thought, a smile curving her lips. How they managed to look after themselves she would never know, but there seemed to be no shortage of tinned food in the cupboards, and Bruce had assured her that the restaurant on the corner of their block served an excellent meal which they could afford if they were really hungry, and the laundry across the street took care of their dirty linen and clothes.

Bruce's impatient thumping on the bathroom door made her hurry out of the bath, drying herself vigorously until her skin tingled before she pulled on a bath robe and called to him that the bathroom was vacant.

Less than an hour later Joanne stood glancing at herself critically in the mirror. Green was not always her favourite colour as it invariably clashed with her eyes, but she had been unable to resist this leafy-green chiffon gown with its wide sleeves and delicate lacework at her narrow waist. The effect was altogether pleasing, she decided finally as she swivelled about in front of the tall mirror.

She had left her hair loose for this occasion, something which she rarely did, and it fell softly to her shoulders, the golden-brown sheen accentuated by the light directly above her. About her neck she wore a single string of pearls which had once been her mother's, and matching earrings were fastened to her small ear lobes. She wanted to look her best, she thought happily. It was not often that her brother offered to take her out.

The doorbell chimed loudly as she placed her white silk wrap and evening bag on the foot of the bed, and she was still hesitating as to what to do when Bruce called from the room next to hers.

'Will you answer that, Jo?'

'Were you expecting anyone?' she asked, hovering outside the door.

'Friends often drop in on the off-chance of getting a free beer,' he replied. 'If it's one of those, tell them the cupboard is bare and they'd better scoot.'

Smiling to herself, Joanne crossed the small lounge just as the doorbell chimed impatiently a second time. Whoever it was, they did not like the idea of being kept waiting, she thought, her fingers fumbling with the unfamiliar lock before the door swung open.

The faint smile froze on her lips as she stared up at the man standing on the doorstep.

'You!' she gasped incredulously, her wild glance taking in Daniel's dark evening suit, tailored impeccably to fit that lean, muscular body, and the almost startling contrast of his white shirt front, accentuating the hard arrogance of the tanned face above the black bow-tie. When she managed to still the clamouring of her heart, she demanded hoarsely, 'What are *you* doing here?'

His eyebrows rose mockingly. 'Ungracious as always.'

'I didn't know you intended coming to Cape Town as well,' she remarked carelessly, standing aside for him to enter and experiencing an unwanted quiver of pleasure as he brushed past her in the confined space.

'It slipped my mind,' he said abruptly, his glance going beyond her. 'Oh, hello, Bruce. Did you get those tickets for me?'

'Yes,' Bruce nodded, darting a glance at Joanne as he handed two tickets to Daniel. 'It was the best I could do at such short notice.'

'I'm very much obliged to you,' Daniel smiled, pocketing the tickets and turning to Joanne who had stood by silently, and curiously. 'Are you ready?'

'Ready?' she asked, a little bewildered.

'They're doing *Swan Lake* at the Nico Malan Theatre,' Daniel informed her with a hint of impatience.

'What has that to do with me?' she demanded haughtily, her body inexplicably tense.

'I'm taking you,' he replied with arrogant confidence, tapping his fingers against his jacket pocket. 'Hence the tickets.'

'Just a minute,' Joanne snapped, suspicion flaring like a raw flame within her. 'Was this little escapade planned between the two of you? Is that why I received this unusual invitation to spend the week-end at your flat, Bruce?'

A dull red colour stained Bruce's cheeks. 'Well, I——'

'It was my idea entirely,' Daniel cut in.

'It may have been your idea, but Bruce didn't have to go along with it,' she stated coldly, keeping a tight rein on her anger and disappointment.

Daniel gestured impatiently. 'We're wasting time, Joanne.'

'I don't care how much time we're wasting. I'm not going with you,' she almost shouted.

'Oh, yes, you are.' Hard fingers latched on to her arm, biting cruelly into soft flesh. 'Bruce, get her wrap and her bag, or whatever it is women take with them on an evening out.'

'You can't bully me into going with you, Daniel,' she said through her teeth, struggling to free her arm but only punishing herself in the process.

'I would carry you kicking and screaming down to the car if the need arose,' he threatened harshly, and the gleam in his eyes was a warning to her that he would not hesitate to carry out his threat. Bruce returned with her things and, to her annoyance, Daniel placed her wrap about her shoulders as if she were a child before pressing her bag into her hands. 'Are you ready to come quietly, or do I carry you down?'

The atmosphere seemed to be crackling with electricity as she glanced from Daniel to Bruce, and back. 'I think you're both despicable!'

Bruce coloured with discomfort. 'You're just being difficult, Jo.'

'Difficult!' she almost screamed at him, her eyes dark green pools of anger in her white face. 'The trouble is that neither of you consider that I have any feelings at all. You shove me about as if I were a lifeless sack of potatoes, uncaring whether I'm bruised or hurt in the process.'

'We're sufficiently impressed by your little speech, now come on,' Daniel instructed impatiently. 'I dislike intensely walking into the theatre when the curtain has already risen.'

Choking down her bitterness, she stood by helplessly as Bruce gave Daniel the spare key to the flat before she found herself ushered unceremoniously into the lift which swept them down to the ground floor.

'This way,' said Daniel, guiding her to where his dark green Citroën was parked. 'I'm glad you're being sensible at last.'

Joanne did not reply, choking back the angry words that hovered on her lips and fighting for the control she had lost so completely shortly after his arrival at Bruce's flat.

It did not take them long to arrive at the foreshore where the Nico Malan Theatre was ablaze with lights. It was considered the most modern in the world, and the largest in the southern hemisphere, but Joanne was strangely unimpressed by its splendour as she was whisked through the magnificent foyer and into the opera house where they were promptly shown to their seats.

'Relax, Joanne,' Daniel whispered once they were seated. 'I can feel you vibrating with tension and anger, and I don't find that very complimentary.'

'I feel like clawing your eyes out!' she hissed back at him.

'Here?' he demanded softly, his glance mocking. 'In this lovely theatre?'

Her eyes flashed green sparks of anger. 'I don't very much care where I do it.'

'I suggest you wait until we're alone, then you can claw all you like,' he replied, an undertone of sensuality in his lowered voice. 'I think I might even enjoy being clawed by you.'

'I hate you!' she whispered fiercely, wishing there were not so many people seated about them sending curious glances in their direction.

'You're repeating yourself, and it can become so tiresome.'

'Good!' she replied coldly. 'When I've become too tiresome to bear you may leave me in peace.'

'My darling,' he murmured, his voice a velvet warmth that washed over her and set her disobedient pulses beating rapidly. 'You're so very beautiful when you're angry that I'm finding it extremely difficult not to take you in my arms and kiss you, regardless of all the prying eyes.'

His glance lingered on her lips and it was like a physical contact; a suggestive intimacy. It sent the blood pounding through her veins and surging into her cheeks as she wrenched her glance away from his just as the lights were dimmed and the first haunting strains of Tchaikovsky's *Swan Lake* filled the opera house.

It was not the first time she had seen this particular ballet being performed, but nonetheless she sat spellbound, forgetting almost Daniel's presence beside her as she became entwined in the poignant theme, and sighing almost regretfully when the curtain came down on the final scene.

'I'm glad you enjoyed it,' Daniel remarked, giving her a sidelong glance, and before she could prevent herself, she smiled up at him.

Her nerves were too deliciously untangled to continue doing battle with him, and she offered no resistance when his hand lay warm against her waist as he guided her into the foyer.

'Daniel, darling,' a musical, faintly husky female voice made Daniel tense beside her, his arm almost painfully tight about her waist as they turned to face the woman approaching them from across the crowded foyer. She was a blonde, striking-looking woman in her early thirties, Joanne judged swiftly, and her diamonds glittered almost harshly beneath the expensive lighting. 'I knew I couldn't be mistaken,' she smiled charmingly as she reached their side.

'Greta,' Daniel said in surprise. 'What on earth are you doing in Cape Town? Is Manfred with you?'

'Didn't you know?' she asked dramatically, her cool grey eyes as hard as the diamonds about her slender throat. 'Manfred died about two months ago and, as you know, I was never happy in South West Africa.'

'I'm sorry, I didn't know,' Daniel remarked regretfully before pushing Joanne forward a little. 'Greta, I would like you to meet my ...' Joanne's sharp glance made him pause moments before he uttered the word 'wife'. 'I would like you to meet Joanne Webster. Joanne, this is Greta Neal. Greta and I have known each other since our pre-school days.'

'How do you do, Mrs Neal,' Joanne murmured politely.

The curvaceous body in the black dress and expensive furs seemed to stiffen, the hard eyes speculative as Greta Neal nodded coolly in Joanne's direction before returning her attention to Daniel, switching on her radiance as one would switch on a light.

'Tell me, darling, are you still living here in the Mother City?' she wanted to know, her slender, bejewelled fingers resting possessively on Daniel's arm.

'No,' Daniel replied, a smile curving his lips. 'As a matter of fact, Joanne and I are both working at a clinic in Willowmead.'

'Are you a doctor too?'

Those cold eyes seemed to dissect Joanne quite thoroughly. 'No, Mrs Neal. I'm a nurse.'

'Oh . . .' the scarlet lips curled insultingly.

'Greta, you must excuse us,' Daniel said abruptly, and Joanne could almost feel the impatience ripple through him.

'I hope I shall see you again, darling,' that musical voice almost purred. 'We must talk about the old times, mustn't we?'

'It was nice seeing you again, Greta,' Daniel replied, ignoring the suggestiveness in her remark. Then, nodding coolly, he said 'goodnight' and almost rushed Joanne off her feet in his hurry to reach his car.

'Now don't start panicking,' he said eventually when they passed the turn-off to Bruce's flat. 'I'm taking you somewhere where we can have a quiet drink to round off the evening with.'

It had not occurred to her to offer any protestations, she was far too busy trying to find the appropriate place in Daniel's past for that sparkling blonde who no doubt possessed a heart as hard as her cold grey eyes. Trying to imagine her as a little girl was quite impossible, and trying to picture Daniel as a small boy was equally difficult. Did he ever climb trees? she wondered bemusedly, thinking of those carefree days when her parents had still been alive, and she and Bruce had spent hours climbing the trees in the back garden, pretending to be Tarzan and Jane with some frightful mission to accomplish before the sun set behind the Hottentot's Holland mountains.

Joanne sighed inwardly. Daniel had most probably been a very correct little boy; never too boisterous, and never dirty. Greta Neal could not have been anything other than a prim little doll, she decided, her thoughts jumping back to the woman they had met so unexpectedly that evening. Frills and lace, and fancy ribbons—that was how Joanne saw Greta Neal as a child.

The car turned off the freeway, the lights sweeping the street ahead, and a certain warmth stole through her, relaxing her completely in Daniel's company as she recalled his behaviour in the foyer of the Nico Malan Theatre. He had not been very pleased to see this woman who had swept down upon them like some bird selecting its prey and coming in for the kill. He had been friendly, but cool and aloof, and had so very nearly made it quite plain that she, Joanne, was his wife. If she had not stopped him, Greta Neal would most probably have faded back into the past, but Joanne had a strange feeling that, despite Daniel's reluctance to become involved, they had not seen the last of that woman.

CHAPTER ELEVEN

'TELL me about Greta Neal,' said Joanne after they had been shown to a secluded table at a small but respectable night club just outside the city.

Daniel's lips twisted into a smile as he stared down into the amber-coloured liquid in his glass. 'What would you like to know?'

'Was her husband a farmer in South West?'

'He was in the diamond industry.'

'That figures,' she laughed softly. 'She certainly has more nerve than I would have to wear all that expensive stuff in public. It's like displaying your bank statement to whoever cared to notice.'

'Greta was always one for glittering trinkets, and Manfred pampered her expensive tastes like the fool he was,' Daniel remarked soberly, his strong, clever fingers twirling the glass on the table.

'Were you ever in love with her?'

'Certainly not!' he exploded. 'I did at one stage think she married Manfred in a fit of pique because I made it so obvious that I didn't want her hanging around me, but I was very much a self-opinionated student at the time. Now, of course, I'm sure she married him for all the usual reasons.'

'And he's obviously made her a very wealthy widow ... darling,' she added mischievously, mimicking Greta Neal's voice to perfection.

'You little minx,' he smiled, his hand gripping hers with

155

unexpected firmness across the table, and sending familiar little tremors up the length of her arm.

'You'd better watch out, Daniel. I have a feeling that you're going to be chased,' she teased lightly, amazing even herself that she could all at once be so relaxed in his company.

'To be chased by a woman has never appealed to me,' he replied, making her realise, if she had not done so before, that he was very much a man who did his own chasing. 'Would you like to dance?'

She nodded a little apprehensively and was instantly drawn to her feet and led through the tables towards the space cleared for dancing which was already crowded with couples swaying slowly to the rhythm supplied by the jazz quartet.

'You have enjoyed the evening, haven't you?' he asked softly just above her ear as he steered her expertly amongst the others on the floor.

'Yes,' she whispered back, almost reluctant to break the spell that seemed to have woven itself about her. 'It was silly of me to be so angry. I'm sorry.'

'If I'd extended the invitation in the usual manner, would you have accepted?'

'Probably not,' she replied after a moment of thought.

'Are Bruce and I forgiven, then?'

'Yes.'

His arm tightened about her waist, drawing her against the lean hardness of his body as she matched her steps to his. 'Are you in the mood to say yes to all my suggestions this evening?'

'That depends.'

'On what?' he asked, his warm breath stirring through the fine hair at her temples and awakening a slumbering pulse at the base of her throat.

'It depends on the suggestions you make, naturally.'

He drew his head back slightly. 'You look so beautifully fragile this evening, as if you would melt in my arms.' His glance lingered on her lips where a tiny nerve pulsed at the corner of her mouth. 'I want to kiss you.'

'Not here!' she protested swiftly, her cheeks suffused with colour when the strange glitter in his eyes made her realise what she had said. 'I mean——'

'At my hotel?' he suggested with a warmth that sent the blood racing through her veins.

'No.'

'Where, then?' he demanded softly, his glance teasing.

'Daniel——'

She got no further, for he laughed softly, lowering his head until the hardness of his chin was pressed against her temple. 'I'm in a crazy mood tonight, my Lorelei. Let's pretend, just for this one night, that we find each other attractive, and that we're enjoying each other's company.'

'And then?' she asked softly, her head somehow finding its way on to his shoulder where the expensive material of his jacket was smooth against her cheek.

'Then, my beautiful sea-nymph, we just let nature take its course and see where it leads.'

They danced in silence for a moment before she said: 'This could be a dangerous game you're suggesting.'

'It could also be quite an innocent game, with nothing to lose except a few harmless kisses before I deposit you at Bruce's flat,' he replied in a voice that was vibrantly low.

Her hand tightened on his arm where the muscles were hard beneath her fingers. 'Can I trust you not to take advantage of me while we indulge in this rather foolish game?'

'You can trust me, Joanne, to do nothing you wouldn't want me to do,' he promised, dropping a kiss on her silky hair. 'Are we partners in this crazy game of mine?'

'You're very persuasive, and I *am* tempted,' she replied with honesty, but could she take the risk of involving herself in this game without giving herself away completely?

'Be a devil just this once,' he challenged.

Joanne lifted her head and raised her glance to his, her eyes a soft, velvety green in the subdued light. 'Just this once I'm going to be as crazy as you are, and say ... yes.'

'Wonderful!' he exclaimed softly, almost lifting her off the floor as he swung her round in his arms.

It was like a strange madness gripping Joanne, and the subtle change in Daniel's behaviour encouraged her to drift more deeply into this game of pretence than she had intended to. They laughed and talked and danced until well after midnight, oblivious of the others about them, and somehow not caring that their behaviour might have been thought odd.

Driving back to the flat eventually, Daniel pulled off to the side of the quiet road and switched off the engine before he drew her unresistingly into his arms. His kisses were warm and deeply disturbing, and she found herself caught under the spell of the evening as she kissed him back. In the lift, as it swept them up to Bruce's flat, he kissed her again, then in the flat, with the door closed and shutting them off from the outside world, she found herself in his arms once more.

Perhaps it was the amount of wine she had consumed,

or just the sheer maleness of him that kept her spell-bound, but loving him as she did made it difficult to draw the line between reality and pretence, until the warm pressure of his hands against her breasts warned her that the game would have to end.

She pulled away from him, using her brother as an excuse, but Daniel caught her close once more.

'Bruce is at a party with some of his student pals and, if I remember my own university days, it won't end until the early hours of the morning.' His mouth found the vulnerable pulse in the soft hollow of her throat. 'We have plenty of time.'

'Daniel, it's been a memorable evening. Let's not spoil it,' she pleaded breathlessly, her hands against his chest to ward him off.

'I have no intention of doing anything to spoil our evening together,' he promised, drawing back a little.

'Could we—could we talk? Quietly and calmly, *and* seriously,' she suggested hesitantly, reality returning with a painful force.

'Must we talk now?' he asked, an incredulous smile about his lips as he slid his hands down the length of her arms to her wrists, sending tantalising sparks along her nerves.

'I think so, Daniel,' she nodded slowly. 'We're both quite calm at the moment.'

'I wouldn't say that I'm calm,' he remarked with a certain harshness as he raised her hand and slipped it inside his jacket where she could feel the heavy beat of his heart beneath the silk of his shirt. 'Would my heart beat like that if I were calm?'

'Daniel?' she pleaded, the warmth of his body beneath her hand almost too much to bear.

He released her instantly. 'All right, let's talk if that's what you want.'

His voice had suddenly assumed its usual abruptness as they sat down facing each other in Bruce's untidy lounge, and, for a brief moment, Joanne wondered whether it was wise of her to want to discuss a subject which could quite easily make him revert back to the mocking, arrogant stranger she had come to fear.

'Well?' he demanded softly, his glance compelling.

'Won't you please reconsider and give me a divorce?'

Clearly taken aback, he lit a cigarette, his eyes narrowed against the screen of smoke when he eventually said: 'If you give me a very good reason why I should, then I might consider starting divorce proceedings.'

'I want to make a life for myself somewhere without the past entangling me in its clutches, and I want to continue with my nursing career,' she replied, her words sounding hollow and decidedly flat. 'I can't do that, Daniel, while our marriage hangs over my head like the sword of Damocles.'

The silence lengthened between them, a silence during which she found herself thinking, 'If Daniel cares in any way for me, he'll brush aside my request and suggest again, as he did once before his mother's death, that we seriously consider making something of our marriage.' It was a foolish hope, a ridiculous desire, but she had to put him to the test to make sure.

'Is your freedom so important to you?' he asked finally, his voice grating along her tender nerves.

'Yes, it is,' she lied desperately. 'Very important.'

'And . . . if I give you this divorce you want so badly . . . where will you go?'

'Somewhere quiet,' she announced. 'I hope, to a place

similar to Willowmead.'

His eyebrows rose a fraction. 'You wouldn't stay on at the clinic?'

She shook her head, a wave of silky hair falling forward to cast a shadow across her face. 'It would be better if we don't see each other so often.'

'You would allow me to visit you occasionally?' he asked, an unfathomable urgency in his voice.

'Occasionally, yes. If you felt like doing so.'

A tense silence hovered between them, then Daniel sighed heavily. 'Very well, Joanne. I'll make the necessary arrangements.'

Joanne tasted the bitterness of defeat as she forced a smile to her unwilling lips and whispered, 'Thank you, Daniel.'

'Don't thank me,' he said harshly, crushing his cigarette into the ashtray. 'Thank the mood I'm in. Tomorrow I shall quite probably want to kick myself.'

'I trust you not to go back on your word.'

'I trusted you ... once.'

She lowered her glance swiftly to hide the pain in her eyes. 'I know ... and I let you down.'

'Yes, and—no.' She glanced up quickly, but he was staring at something beyond her with an almost distant look in his eyes. 'I told you, didn't I? Up there in the Alps there was plenty of time to think, and to remember.' His blue gaze sharpened as it met hers. 'You did let me down, but somehow you never let Mother down. That's the mystifying part of it. She *was* happy about us—right up to the end.'

'Yes,' she managed, her throat tightening.

He leaned forward in his chair, his knees almost touching hers. 'Did you give her the idea that you wanted our marriage to become a real one?'

His guess was so accurate that it took almost everything Joanne possessed not to let him see the truth; the humiliating, utterly hopeless truth.

'Your—your mother had guessed the truth about our marriage almost before I had the opportunity to tell her. She drew her own conclusions, and I—I didn't deny it.'

'My God!' he muttered, rising to his feet and walking away from her, the muscles in his jaw standing out prominently. 'How you must hate me for what happened afterwards!'

Long after he had gone, his words still remained with her. 'How you must hate me for what happened afterwards!'

She *had* hated him, yes, for taking her in what she had thought a brutal fashion. But hate is akin to love, and love had made her heart forgiving when she had realised that her pride had been bruised most. If one word of love had passed his lips, she would not have left him, but then, as now, Daniel merely desired her body, as he would desire any other woman under similar circumstances, and she shrank from a relationship with Daniel which was based purely on the physical. When the flame had spent itself, only the ashes would remain, and ashes was not a recommended diet for a hungry heart.

Spring had come to the valley with a gentleness that brought it to life magically. The vineyards below the clinic became a carpet of green as the sap rose to produce new shoots in preparation for another season of wine-making. In the clinic gardens the daffodils and namaqualand daisies raised their heads proudly towards the sun while the gardeners loosened the soil and planted seedlings for the coming summer.

Joanne, returning from the canteen where she had indulged in a hasty lunch, paused for a moment to admire the scene before her, enjoying too the warmth of the sun against her face and arms before she mounted the steps and entered the building through the reception hall, coming almost face to face with Daniel and Greta Neal.

'Well, if it isn't the little nurse I saw you with just over a week ago,' she purred beside Daniel, but the eyes that met Joanne's were cold and hard. 'Will you be taking care of me while I'm here?'

Bewildered, Joanne stared at her for a moment before casting a swift, questioning glance at Daniel.

'Sister Webster is in the theatre, Greta,' he answered for Joanne in an abrupt, gravelly voice that matched the scowl on his face.

Greta Neal, the inevitable fur draped across her shoulders, and her diamond earrings matching the diamond pendant at her throat, placed a slender, manicured hand on Daniel's arm. It signified a possessiveness that made Joanne almost choke with an uncommon jealousy.

'I was hoping we could get to know each other,' Greta Neal was saying, but despite the smile on her crimson lips, Joanne experienced a flash of warning. This woman was out to cause trouble of some sort while she staked her claim on her childhood friend, Daniel Grant.

Daniel took her arm with a gesture of impatience and with a polite nod in Joanne's direction, he ushered Greta down the wide passage. Stunned and puzzled, Joanne glanced at the girl behind the reception desk.

'Is Mrs Neal going to be a patient here in the clinic?'

'Yes,' the dark-haired girl nodded, grasping at the unexpected opportunity to discuss the new arrival. 'She arrived about thirty minutes ago in a chauffeur-driven car, insisting that she wanted to see Dr Grant, and no one else.'

A puzzled frown creased Joanne's brow. 'What special surgery could she possibly require that would bring her here to this clinic?'

'Apparently she has a mole on her left shoulder that she wants removed.'

'A mole?' Joanne asked in amazement. 'But the removal of a mole could have been done just as expertly in a Cape Town hospital. Why come here?'

The receptionist giggled. 'That's what Dr Grant told her, but she said, and I quote, "Darling, I wouldn't let anyone else but you lay a finger on my mole," unquote.' Her reproduction of Greta Neal's particular way of speaking made Joanne smother a laugh behind her hand. 'You should have seen Dr Grant's face,' the receptionist continued, rolling her eyes towards the ceiling. 'I've never seen him look so angry before, and if I'd been Mrs Neal, I would have got out fast, but she merely caught him in the beam of her flashing smile and produced the necessary papers from her personal doctor. It had all been arranged, and there was nothing Dr Grant could do about it except remove her infernal mole and be done with it.'

The girl's dislike of Greta Neal was evident, and Joanne could not blame her, for that was exactly how she felt herself, she thought as she made her way towards the theatre wing.

Greta Neal was wheeled into the theatre during the course of the following day and, to Joanne's surprise, Daniel treated this minor operation with as much care as if he were remodelling someone's maimed features.

'My personal feelings don't come into it,' he explained

that evening when he arrived unexpectedly at Joanne's flat. 'On the operating table she was just another patient, and her unnecessary request was of no importance at all.'

'How long will she be staying?' Joanne asked, avoiding his glance with care.

'She could return home tomorrow, but, knowing Greta, she'll most probably make an occasion out of her stay at the clinic.' He snorted angrily. 'When I left the clinic fifteen minutes ago, she was complaining of a weakness that prevented her from getting up and seeing to herself.'

Joanne swallowed nervously. 'You mean she's going to stretch out her stay here for as long as possible?'

'She'll stay until I virtually have to throw her out.' Daniel pressed his fingers against his eyes for a moment. 'Heavens, but I'm tired tonight!'

Joanne observed him closely for a moment, seeing for the first time the tiredness etched so deeply in his features, and the dullness in the eyes that finally blinked up at her as he leaned back in his chair.

'I'll make you something to drink, then I suggest you go home to bed,' she said sympathetically as she went through to the kitchen to switch on the kettle.

Some minutes later when she returned to the lounge with their coffee, she found his jacket and tie draped across the arm of the chair he had been seated in, but Daniel was nowhere in sight and, placing the cups on the low table, she made her way hesitantly towards her room.

Daniel lay sprawled across her bed, and it gave her the strangest feeling to see him there in her room with his arms flung out to his sides and his features relaxed in sleep. He looked almost boyish, she thought, her hungry glance dwelling on his thick lashes, and the dark hair which lay across his broad forehead. Her hand went out automatically to brush it back, but she drew back sharply without touching him, her heart pounding uncomfortably when she realised what she had almost done.

Joanne did not have the heart to wake him and, covering him lightly with a rug, she returned quietly to the lounge to drink her coffee in silence while she settled down to the mending of some of her summer dresses which Daniel had interrupted with his unexpected arrival. It was after ten before she returned to her room with a fresh cup of coffee in her hand to awaken him.

'Daniel,' she whispered, touching his arm gently.

'Lorelei,' he murmured, opening his eyes and throwing aside the rug as he swung his long legs off the side of the bed. 'I wish you wouldn't tie your hair up in that ridiculous ponytail,' he admonished her, drawing her down beside him and tugging at the ribbon until her hair fell down to her shoulders. 'That looks so much better.'

'I've brought you a fresh cup of coffee, then you must go home,' she said, her voice level despite his disturbing touch.

'Did I fall asleep?'

'Yes,' she gestured towards the clock on the bedside table. 'It's after ten.'

A mocking smile touched his lips. 'How unsociable of me!'

'You were tired,' she reminded him woodenly, shutting her mind to the sensations created by the touch of his hand on her hair.

'So you left me sleeping here on your bed.' His hand fastened on to the nape of her neck, while the other lay warm against her waist as he pushed her over backwards on to the bed. 'It's a very comfortable bed, too.'

He stilled her protests with his lips, systematically

breaking down her resistance until she allowed him to coax her lips apart with his own. The hands she had raised with which to ward him off, relaxed against his muscular shoulders, making little caressing movements as he continued to arouse her emotions with an expertise that left her weak and trembling in his arms.

'Daniel, it's late,' she pleaded eventually, her voice sounding choked as his lips trailed a path of destruction along her neck to her shoulder.

'You wouldn't consider letting me stay?'

'What do you think people would say when news gets around that your car was parked outside my flat all night?'

'I could always wave our marriage certificate under their noses,' he announced mockingly before his lips met hers in another soul-destroying kiss. 'Do I stay?'

'No, Daniel,' she insisted, clinging to her sanity. 'I'm not interested in that kind of relationship with you.'

'What kind of relationship *are* you interested in?' he mocked, his eyes dark and searching as they met hers. 'A platonic relationship that allows a few kisses, a little bit of petting, but definitely no sex?'

'Daniel!' she gasped, her cheeks suffused with colour as she fought against him, but his arms tightened mercilessly about her.

'There have been occasions, my little ice-maiden, when I could have sworn that you wanted me as much as I wanted you, and this is one of them. If we weren't married, I would have understood your reluctance, but we are married, and I have made love to you once before.'

'In one hell of a way, yes!' she cried out, anger coming to her rescue.

'I was unforgivably angry that night,' he acknowledged

with a harsh twist of his lips, but his hands moved persuasively against her back. 'Let me show you that making love can be pleasurable as well.'

'No!'

'I'm not going to hurt you,' he murmured, his voice thick with passion, his breath warm against her throat.

'Let me go!' she begged, her heart hammering wildly beneath his hands as she tried to twist herself free of him, but he released her suddenly and she jumped to her feet, the quick rise and fall of her breasts conveying the extent of her disturbed emotions.

'Sit down beside me while I drink my coffee. I'm not going to bite you,' he instructed, gripping her wrist and pulling her down beside him again. He drained his cup of coffee within a few seconds and, replacing it in the saucer, he turned to face her, his eyes hard and strangely cold as they bore into hers. 'One day soon, Joanne, you and I must have a talk, a serious talk for both our sakes, but it will have to keep for the time being.'

He rose without a word and went through to the lounge to collect his jacket and tie, and Joanne followed more slowly, her legs trembling to such an extent that she found herself gripping the back of a chair for support.

'Thank you for your hospitality,' he said cynically, shrugging himself into his jacket and pushing his tie into the pocket. 'Perhaps it wasn't such a good idea to come here this evening after all.'

'Daniel,' she managed to find her voice as he reached the door, but it was thin and wavery. 'Perhaps what we both need is our freedom.'

His lips tightened perceptibly. 'I'm beginning to think you're right.'

The front door slammed behind him with such a force

that the windows rattled, and a few moments later Joanne heard the Citroën being driven away at a tremendous speed. She remained where she was until she could no longer hear it, then reaction set in and the tears made their way silently down her cheeks.

The telephone rang on Joanne's desk just as she was about to go to lunch the following day and, frowning slightly, she lifted the receiver.

'When you have a free moment, Sister Webster, come along to ward 421,' Sister Dawson's voice came over the line. 'Mrs Neal wishes to speak to you quite urgently.'

'I'll come at once, Sister,' Joanne replied, wondering at the note of irritation in the ward Sister's voice.

'What's the problem?' Alice asked curiously, pulling a face when Joanne mentioned Greta Neal's name. 'She's had the staff running round in circles ever since her arrival two days ago, I believe. Is she a special friend of Dr Grant's?'

'I wouldn't know,' Joanne replied evasively as she prepared to leave her office.

'Rumour has it that there might be wedding bells in the near future,' Alice persisted, and Joanne's heart lurched uncomfortably.

'You shouldn't listen to gossip, Alice,' she reprimanded more sharply than was necessary. 'And most important of all, you shouldn't repeat what you hear.'

Ignoring Alice's surprised glance, she turned on her heel and left the room, making her way along the wide passages to Greta Neal's ward, her soft-soled shoes making no sound on the tiled floor.

'So you came at last,' Greta Neal's husky voice accused when Joanne entered her ward. 'I've been trying to contact you all day.'

'I've been in the theatre most of the morning, Mrs Neal.'

'With Daniel?'

Her cold eyes sliced through Joanne, who felt her body grow tense. 'With Dr Grant, and several other surgeons who happened to be operating today.'

The blonde head tilted enquiringly, while slender fingers played idly with the wide collar of the lacy bed-jacket. 'What is there between yourself and Daniel?'

Joanne stared at her in bewilderment. 'I beg your pardon?'

'You heard me,' Greta snapped, her crimson lips twisting into a firm line.

'Really, Mrs Neal,' Joanne remarked coldly. 'Was this why you asked me to come and see you?'

'Answer my question,' Greta gestured impatiently, the diamond ring on her finger catching the light from the window. 'What is there between the two of you?'

Joanne clenched her hands tightly behind her back as she fought to keep her anger in check. 'There's nothing between Dan—Dr Grant and myself.'

Greta Neal missed nothing, and her eyes narrowed perceptibly at Joanne's faltering statement. 'What is this hold that you have over him, then? Are you his mistress?'

Joanne stared hard at the woman who reclined so elegantly in the high hospital bed, and wondered where this conversation was heading. 'I'm afraid I don't know what you're talking about.'

Those crimson lips curved into a smile, but it never reached Greta's eyes. 'I know men well enough, darling, and, considering that you spent the week-end together in Cape Town, you must have some hold over him.'

'I did not spend the week-end with Dr Grant, I——'

'I want him, Sister Webster,' Greta stated quite firmly, the husky quality in her voice enchanced by her determination. 'And I don't intend that there should be any opposition, so name your price.'

Joanne felt as though a douche of cold water had been dashed into her face. 'My—*price*?'

'Yes,' the grey eyes studied her thoughtfully as if assessing her worth. 'Would two thousand Rand be enough to make you stay away from him?'

'Two thousand?' Joanne gasped, suppressing the hysteria that rose to the surface within her. It was unbelievable! Greta Neal was offering her money to leave Daniel alone; to leave her own husband alone. 'Mrs Neal, I think you're making a mistake, I——'

'Five thousand, then,' Greta pushed up her price, her face a mask of cold hatred. 'I should have known that a slut like yourself wouldn't be satisfied with less.'

Joanne paled visibly, her eyes dark green pools of anger as she forced the words past her unwilling lips. 'Mrs Neal, if this was all you asked me to come here for, then you must excuse me. I have work to do.'

Greta Neal sat up in bed, her body quivering and her hands clutching agitatedly at the sheets. 'I demand an answer!'

'You are not in a position to demand anything of me, Mrs Neal,' Joanne said coldly, sickened by their conversation. 'I don't want your money, and neither do I intend answering your outrageous questions.'

CHAPTER TWELVE

JOANNE'S heart was pounding in her ears as she made her way back to her office. Never in her life had she been so insulted, nor felt as degraded as she felt at that moment, she thought angrily. The entire episode had sickened her to the core. Greta Neal could have Daniel for all she cared. Who knows, they might just suit each other.

'Joanne!' The object of her thoughts appeared around the first corner, his hands digging into her shoulders as his perceptive glance went down the passage to Greta Neal's ward. 'What were you doing in Greta's ward?'

'Why don't you ask *her*?' she replied fiercely, trying to twist herself free, but failing.

'I'm asking *you*, Joanne,' Daniel stated firmly, then, glancing into the empty office across the passage, he pushed her inside and closed the door. 'Now, tell me.'

She caught her lip between her teeth until it hurt as she made an effort to steady herself, and decided that it was perhaps best that Daniel should know exactly what had occurred. 'Mrs Neal seemed to think I had some sort of hold over you, and offered me money to stay out of your way.'

Daniel stared at her for a moment in stunned surprise, then threw back his head and laughed loudly, obviously finding the whole thing amusing. 'What did you say to that?' he asked when he was able to control himself.

'I very nearly told her to go to the devil!' she retorted angrily, then, calming herself, she said: 'Daniel, that woman means trouble, and I have a terrible feeling that her venom is aimed at me personally.'

'You're imagining things, Joanne,' he told her seriously. 'If I were you, I would ignore what's just happened. There's nothing Greta could possibly do to harm you.'

'I hope you're right, that's all I can say,' she sighed, but that niggling suspicion persisted during the rest of that day, and the following, until she felt like a tightly coiled spring ready to snap at the least little thing.

'Sister Webster, Mrs Neal wishes to see you,' Sister Dawson informed her on the telephone the moment she had returned from her lunch-hour.

'I'm afraid I can't make it today,' Joanne evaded the request. 'We have had a tight schedule this morning, and this afternoon——' She hesitated, her thoughts darting nervously in several directions. 'Tell Mrs Neal I'm sorry, but it's out of the question.'

'She won't like it,' Sister Dawson warned irritably. 'I'm having enough trouble with her as it is.'

Joanne felt sympathetic towards the ward Sister, but was determined not to be swayed from her decision. 'Mrs Neal is too used to having her own way, but she won't succeed with me.'

Later that afternoon a young ward nurse handed Joanne a small white envelope, and the expensive perfume clinging to it told her instantly from whom it came. Avoiding Alice's curious glance, she slid the point of her scissors beneath the flap and ripped it open.

'Sister Webster,' the flowery handwriting began, 'If you don't want the entire hospital to know that you spent the week-end with Daniel, I suggest you pay me a visit during the course of the afternoon. Greta Neal.'

Joanne felt herself go cold as she ripped the short note

into tiny pieces and dropped them into the bin beside her
desk.

'Mrs Neal again?' Alice guessed shrewdly, and when
Joanne nodded, 'I really don't know why you allow that
woman to get under your skin this way.'

Joanne smiled briefly, trying to banish her own fears.
'Will you hold the fort for me while I go along and see
what she wants this time?'

'Of course,' Alice smiled broadly, waving her on her
way.

Joanne was not surprised to find Greta Neal in bed
instead of walking about, or seated in the comfortable
chair which had been provided. Medically speaking she
was well enough to have gone home the day after the removal of her mole, but Greta Neal was the kind of
woman who would make the most of such a situation,
she recalled Daniel's remark, and her wealth contributed
to her behaviour.

'Ah, I see you decided to be sensible about it after all,'
she greeted Joanne, her voice deceptively sweet.

'You left me very little choice, Mrs Neal,' Joanne replied stiffly, venturing no further than the foot of the iron
bed.

'My dear girl, all I wanted to do was apologise for my
behaviour yesterday.' Greta smiled again at Joanne's look
of surprise. 'Do you find it so strange that I should wish
to do so in person?'

'No, I don't really.'

'I said some dreadful things to you, and I do apologise,'
that melodious voice persisted, but to Joanne it was like
a sugar-coated pill with a core of bitterness.

'That's all right, Mrs Neal,' she murmured, suspicious
of this sudden change of attitude, but Greta's perfect

features lit up in a smile of satisfaction.

'Well, now that I have that off my chest ...' She fidgeted against the pillows and glanced helplessly at Joanne. 'I don't suppose that, while you're here, you could do something about these pillows of mine? They're terribly uncomfortable.'

'Yes, of course,' Joanne said politely, Greta's expensive perfume hovering about her as she shifted the pillows into a more comfortable position and straightened the sheets. 'Is that better?'

'Much better, thank you,' that hard mouth curved into a smile. 'Now, I wonder——' She glanced at the bedside cupboard and broke off sharply, her eyes wide and anxious. 'My ring! My diamond ring! It's gone!'

Joanne's nerves quivered at the sound of Greta's raised voice. 'Calm yourself, Mrs Neal. It must be here somewhere.'

'It was here on the cupboard before you came.'

'Perhaps it fell on the floor,' Joanne suggested, going down on her heels.

'Don't be an idiot, I would have heard it if it had fallen,' Greta shrieked. 'It's a very valuable ring. It *must* be found. Do you understand? It must be found!'

Joanne glanced at her in alarm. 'Mrs Neal——'

'Call the Matron. Call Daniel. I want them here, and at once, do you hear!'

'What on earth is going on here?' Sister Dawson demanded as she marched into the ward and found Joanne practically on her hands and knees while she searched the floor in vain, then, rising to her feet, Joanne faced the dark-haired, stern-looking ward Sister.

'Would you ask Matron to come here at once, and try to contact Dr Grant as well.' She gestured towards the blonde, cold-eyed woman in the bed. 'Mrs Neal has lost her diamond ring.'

Sister Dawson closed her eyes as if this was the last straw, but she left the ward immediately to do as Joanne had asked.

As they waited, Joanne searched the floor once more, as well as the bedside cupboard and the bed. She searched in every conceivable place, but the ring was nowhere to be seen, and she had her hands full trying to calm the shrieking, agitated Greta Neal until she was sorely tempted to administer a stinging slap to that lovely face in order to quieten her.

'What the devil is all this fuss about?' Daniel demanded when he finally strode into the ward with Matron following in his wake.

'Daniel!' Greta cried dramatically. 'My diamond ring! It's gone, I tell you!'

'For goodness' sake, Greta,' Daniel scowled. 'Are you certain you haven't put it away somewhere and forgotten about it?'

'No, no, no!' she insisted, gesturing theatrically. 'I took it off and put it down on this cupboard. There,' she indicated with a scarlet-tipped finger towards the spot where she had left it. 'I used some hand lotion and then—and then Sister Webster arrived. I asked her to fix my pillows after a while, and then, when I looked for it, it was gone.'

Matron swung round to face Joanne, her glance stern, 'Have you searched the room, Sister Webster?'

'Yes, Matron,' Joanne replied, her head throbbing.

'Mrs Neal,' Matron continued, turning her attention to the other woman, 'did you say that your ring was on the bedside cupboard just before Sister Webster arrived?'

'Yes, that is so,' Greta replied adamantly, her glance

sweeping Joanne's still figure at the foot of the bed.

'Did anyone else enter this room?' Matron persisted sternly.

'No ... only,' she halted, her glance resting on Joanne, who began to feel the trickle of ice flowing through her veins as she saw the pure vindictiveness sparking from those grey eyes before their owner shrieked, pointing her long, slender finger at Joanne, 'Matron! Search her! Search Sister Webster! She's the only one——'

'Are you out of your mind, Greta?' Daniel interrupted harshly, while Joanne felt as though every drop of blood had been drained from her arteries to leave her rigid and cold.

'Daniel,' Greta continued hysterically, 'I'm telling you that Sister Webster was the only one to enter this ward from the time I removed my ring, until I discovered that it was gone, and I insist that she be searched.'

'Well, really!' Matron muttered uncomfortably, her portly figure quivering with indignation. 'I have never had the unpleasant task of searching anyone before.'

'If the ring has been stolen, then *she* is the only one who could have taken it,' Greta insisted harshly. 'And she must still have it on her.'

'Sister Webster, would you ... er .. .' Matron turned towards Joanne who stood pale and silent beside her. 'Would you turn out your pockets, please.'

'Don't ask *her* to do it,' Greta shrieked indignantly. '*You* do it!'

'Really, Mrs Neal!' Matron objected, but Joanne was only vaguely aware of Matron's blue-uniformed figure beside her as she met Daniel's searching glance. She tried to look away, but couldn't, finding herself unable to obey the silent command in his probing blue gaze. How *could* she defend herself, when everything Greta Neal had said was the truth? She *was* the only person to enter her ward, despite the fact that she had no knowledge at all of the ring's presence on the bedside cupboard. Daniel glanced away suddenly, nodding in Matron's direction, and Joanne spent a few degrading seconds while Matron slid her hands over her body, and finally searched her pockets.

The room was all at once filled with a deathly silence, and, by the look on Matron's face, Joanne knew, even before she spoke, that she had found the missing ring.

She held it up for inspection, allowing the light from the window to sparkle on the stone. 'Is this your ring, Mrs Neal?'

'Yes! Oh, yes!' Greta exclaimed excitedly, but Joanne felt as though she had been winded by an unexpected blow as she met Daniel's cold glance and saw the ominous tightening of the muscles in his jaw. 'How could you, Sister Webster! I never thought of you as a common little thief,' Greta accused, but Joanne was past caring as she saw those slender hands clutch at Daniel's arm to claim his attention. 'Daniel, I insist that you have her dismissed instantly!'

There was a brief pause before Daniel said with forced calmness, 'I think, Greta, you should put on something decent, and accompany us to Matron's office where we can thrash this out quietly and calmly . . . and in private.'

'But I'm ill,' Greta protested, sagging against the pillows. 'I can't——'

'Get up, and do as you're told,' Daniel instructed with harsh abruptness.

'Oh, very well,' she agreed grudgingly, her lips petulant as Matron helped her into her silk robe and slippers.

Joanne felt completely numbed, her legs moving auto-

matically as the four of them made their way silently to
Matron's office and closed the door behind them. Her
premonition had been correct about Greta Neal, but she
had never dreamed that she would go to such lengths to
reach her goal. For a nursing Sister to be accused of theft
was one of the worst things that could happen to anyone, and it was happening to *her*. She had never so much
as stolen a hair from someone's head, but she knew with
painful certainty that Greta Neal was completely aware of
how that ring came to be in her pocket, and it did not
need a psycho-analyst to tell her that this woman would
not admit the truth easily.

'Greta, I want you to think very carefully about this,'
said Daniel once Matron had seated herself behind her
desk, and Greta had subsided gracefully into a chair.
'Was there any way your ring could have fallen into
Sister Webster's pocket without either of you realising
this?'

'There was no way at all,' Greta confirmed, glancing
from the man towering over her to where Joanne stood
stiffly beside Matron's desk. Then her scornful glance
swung back to him. 'For heaven's sake, darling, why
should you try to cover up for her? She's a thief, and
that's all there is to it.'

Daniel's expression hardened as he squared his shoulders and thrust his clenched fists into the pockets of his
white coat. 'Greta, I must make this very clear. Joanne
Webster is not a thief, and I can vouch for that.'

It was like watching some macabre scene in a third-
rate play, Joanne thought wildly, only this time she was
the central character who was having her reputation
ripped to shreds.

'Dr Grant,' Matron interrupted politely, 'may I ask

Sister Webster a few questions?'

'Certainly, Matron,' he inclined his head slightly, glancing at Joanne as Matron began to speak.

'Sister Webster, have you any idea how that ring came to be in your pocket?'

'No idea at all, Matron.'

'Did you notice it on the bedside cupboard when you entered Mrs Neal's room?'

'No, I didn't,' she replied tonelessly.

'She's lying!' Greta spat out the words. 'She saw it, and she must have realised it was an extremely valuable item. That's why she took it.'

'Control yourself, Greta!' Daniel warned sharply, returning his glance to Joanne, who felt herself begin to shake. 'Was there no one else in the ward with you? Someone who may have considered playing a prank on you?'

'Only Sister Dawson,' Joanne replied, licking her dry lips. 'But she came no further than the door.'

'Sister Webster, is there anything you could say in your defence?' Matron intervened, her stern features offering Joanne no comfort.

She shook her head helplessly. 'I can only swear that I never touched Mrs Neal's ring, and I had no idea it was in my pocket.'

Greta gestured impatiently. 'Matron, it's as obvious as the nose on my face that she stole my ring, and I insist that you dismiss her at once.'

'Matron will do nothing of the kind,' Daniel intervened abruptly. 'There must be a reasonable explanation for your ring turning up in Sister Webster's pocket, and I intend to make it my business to go over this whole business step by step until we know exactly what happened.'

'Dr Grant, you seem very certain of Sister Webster's innocence,' Matron frowned up at him. 'May I ask why?'

'There are two reasons why, Matron,' Daniel remarked, a smile touching his lips that sent a quiver of apprehension through Joanne. 'Firstly, I've known Joanne for some years now, and her integrity is something I've always admired. Secondly——'

'Daniel ... please!' Joanne begged hoarsely as she guessed Daniel's intention, and visualised her future lying shattered before her.

'Secondly,' he continued grimly, ignoring her urgent plea, 'Joanne is my wife.'

The axe fell with shattering results. Matron's portly figure in the distinctive blue uniform seemed to expand, the strength of the buttons over her bosom severely tested, while her mouth dropped open, accentuating the double chin. But it was the glittering fury in Greta Neal's eyes that made the blood recede once more from Joanne's cheeks to leave her deathly pale and shaking in every limb.

'You're lying to save her skin!' Greta's voice sparked across the electrified silence.

'On the contrary, Greta,' Daniel smiled lazily, 'I've found the truth a wonderful weapon at times.'

'Then you're a fool!' she snapped, a dull red colour surging up beneath her pale skin. 'I could have offered you so much more.'

'I've never been interested in what you had to offer, Greta, and I never shall be,' he replied without compunction, his cold glance shattering Greta's confidence momentarily. 'For once in your life tell the truth. Clear my wife's name, then you'll at least regain my respect.'

'You win, Daniel,' she replied after a stifling pause,

an affected smile curving her lips as she glanced at the now astonished Matron. 'Yes, I planted my diamond ring in her pocket while she was straightening my sheets and fixing my pilows.'

'But why, Mrs Neal?'

'Why?' Greta laughed, her scornful glance raking Joanne's silent figure. ' I wanted to discredit her in Dr Grant's eyes. I didn't know, of course, that they were already married.'

'No one here at Willowmead knew that Joanne is my wife, Greta,' Daniel told her quietly. 'And no one would have known if you hadn't forced me to make it known in order to protect Joanne.'

'Well, well, well,' she smiled sarcastically. 'So I scored a hit after all. But the damage is done, darling, and I can't say I regret it.' She rose elegantly, her manner indicating that she had regained her composure swiftly. 'I presume I have the authority to discharge myself from this infernal place?'

Daniel nodded. 'You may do so with my compliments.'

'Darling, you're so kind,' she purred, sending a sweeping glance across the room. 'Good day, everyone.'

The door closed behind her moments later, leaving behind only a waft of her perfume as a reminder of her presence as Joanne closed her eyes for a moment and swallowed violently at the desire to be physically sick.

'Sister Webster—I mean, Mrs Grant,' Matron stumbled self-consciously over her words, a new glimmer of respect in her glance that made no impact on Joanne. 'You realise, I suppose, that we cannot allow you to remain in our employ, considering that Dr Grant is your—husband. It's quite unethical, if you'll forgive me for saying so, Dr Grant.'

'Please, Matron,' Joanne interrupted jerkily. There was a limit to what she could take, and she had reached her limit several seconds ago. 'I understand only too well what this means. You shall have my resignation on your desk in the morning. If—if some arrangement could be made for Sister Forbes to take over in the theatre, I—I would like to go home.'

Not waiting for a reply, she walked blindly from Matron's office, her head held high, her back rigid and aching. She could not relax now, she thought as she made her way towards her office to collect her bag before leaving the building. To relax at that moment would be disastrous and embarrassing in front of so many prying eyes, and she had had enough of the enforced limelight.

In the privacy of her flat, Joanne flung her bag across her bed and followed it almost immediately, lying face down across the pillows as she felt the tension snap within her until her shoulders began to shake as painful sobs tore through her slender frame. She wept bitter agonising tears until her pillow was drenched, and she was aware of nothing but an emptiness that left her listless and weak. Her brain felt numb and devoid of thoughts when she eventually made her way into the kitchen to make herself a strong cup of tea. Adding plenty of sugar, she finally sipped at the hot liquid, the shiver coursing its way through her making her realise how cold she was as her composure gradually returned.

There was plenty to do, she decided eventually, but first she had to write out her letter of resignation. Afterwards? Well, that was up to the authorities at the clinic, for there was no longer any place for her there.

Taking her writing case from the shelf in her wardrobe,

Joanne sat down in the lounge and calmly composed the letter of resignation she had promised Matron. When she eventually sealed the envelope, her glance fell on the letter written by Serena Grant shortly before her death, and the contents, which she knew off by heart, were like the thrust of a sword in an open wound. Then, thrusting aside her thoughts, she rose and went through to the kitchen once more to make herself something to eat. The thought of food made her feel ill, but she had to keep busy in order to stop herself from thinking of the past and the future as it mingled to become a grotesque nightmare that threatened to plague her waking thoughts.

Somehow she managed to get through the hours until darkness fell. Then, with nothing more to do, an unnatural coldness gripped her, making her teeth chatter until she finally soaked herself in a hot bath and felt the tension uncoil within her, the warmth of the water soothing the aching muscles along her spine.

She rubbed herself vigorously afterwards, removing the pins from her hair, and wrapping herself in a blue silk robe before she pushed her feet into her soft mules. She emerged from the bathroom moments later, her steps faltering as Daniel's tall figure emerged from the armchair in the lounge. He had obviously made himself at home, for he had removed his jacket and tie, the top buttons of his white shirt undone to display a large portion of his tanned chest.

His glance flickered strangely as it slid down the length of her, making her aware of the fact that she had nothing on beneath that robe, and painfully conscious of her shiny, flushed face. He smiled as if something in her appearance satisfied him.

'I knocked, but you obviously didn't hear me, so I

tried the door, and found it unlocked.'

'What do you want?' she demanded, her voice sounding flat to her own ears as her hands went instinctively towards the belt of her robe to tighten it.

'There are a few things I want to discuss with you.'

'We have nothing to discuss with each other.'

'Oh, yes, we have,' he corrected smoothly. 'First of all, you'll be happy to know that Greta has left the clinic.'

'It doesn't matter any more,' she replied dully, lowering her glance to the floor, and fixing her attention on the intricate pattern of the carpet.

'It matters to me,' Daniel insisted harshly, his polished shoes coming into her line of vision. 'I've never found it very comfortable having her hanging about my neck.'

A little thrill of pleasure made its way through her, but she suppressed it instantly. 'I suppose I should say "thank you" for the way you stood by me this afternoon.'

She heard the rumble of laughter in his throat at her ungraciousness. 'You don't have to if you'd rather not.'

Her head shot up instantly, green sparks of anger flashing from her eyes. 'There was no need for you to mention the fact that we were married.'

'There was every need,' he insisted abruptly, his fingers closing about her arm like a vice as he shook her slightly. 'I'm tired of playing games in an effort to sort out the mess our lives are in.'

'You're hurting my arm.'

'I'm sorry.' He released her instantly, slipping his hand into the pocket of his pants and producing a letter she would have given the world for him not to have seen. 'Why did you never show me this letter?'

'Where did you find it?' she wanted to know, her breath quickening with anxiety.

'There on the sofa,' he indicated her writing case which she had carelessly left open. 'I couldn't help recognising my mother's handwriting,' he continued, his compelling glance capturing hers. 'How long have you had this letter?'

'Sister Johnson gave it to me after the funeral.'

'And you never thought to show it to me?' he accused, dropping the letter on to the sofa beside her writing case.

Stifled by his nearness, she walked across to the window and pushed aside the curtain to stare down into the darkened street below where she could only just make out the shape of his car parked at the curb.

'I wanted to . . . once,' she admitted listlessly. 'But you never gave me much opportunity to explain how it came about.'

'Joanne . . . I must know,' he said directly behind her, and the curtain fell into place as the warmth of his hands on her shoulders seemed to scorch her through the thin silk of her robe. 'Did Mother *suppose* you . . . cared for me? Or did you actually tell her so?'

'I must go and get dressed,' she evaded his questioning, but his hands merely tightened on her shoulders as he swung her round to face him.

'I must know,' he repeated, his glance searching her face.

'Does it matter?'

'Very much.'

Joanne swallowed with difficulty, every nerve in her body aware of his nearness, his touch, and the humiliating admission she could no longer evade. Her throat tightened, making her voice sound like a croak as she said: 'I told her.'

'And you meant it?' he asked softly, the urgency within him conveyed through the slight tremor in his hands.

'Yes,' she admitted, humiliating herself completely as she eventually twisted away from him. 'Well? Why aren't you laughing? It's the joke of the century that I should have been fool enough to fall in love with you.'

His hands reached out for her, drawing her up against him relentlessly. 'How can I laugh, my darling Lorelei, when I've loved you almost from the first time I saw you?'

'Don't ... please,' she begged brokenly, unable to believe him when he had always declared so firmly that he did not believe in love. 'Haven't I shamed myself enough?'

'Joanne, look at me,' he instructed with gentle firmness.

'I can't,' she whispered, her cheeks aflame, her heart pounding in her ears.

'I refuse to talk to the top of your head, pretty as it is,' he laughed, placing his hands on either side of her face and forcing her to meet his eyes; eyes that seemed to be burning with the intensity of his feelings. 'Darling ice-maiden, from the moment I looked into your cool green eyes I knew I intended to marry you some day. I had no intention of rushing you, but, to satisfy my mother, I took her with me to that Christmas dance at the hospital before our marriage.' He smiled with gentle reminiscence. 'I told her that, after my duty dance with the Matron, I would point out my future wife by asking her to dance with me.'

Joanne studied him with a quick ache in her throat as she recalled how he had approached her that night and had asked her to dance. She recalled, too, catching a glimpse of Serena Grant at Matron's table, and knew now why his mother had seemed so familiar that first night when Daniel had taken her to his home in Constantia.

'Joanne,' his lips brushed across her fluttering eyelashes before lingering tenderly on her quivering mouth. 'Our marriage was at the wrong time, and for all the wrong reasons, but I do love you.'

She stared up at him for a moment, afraid to believe him while everything within her clamoured in response to his admission, and it was then that she realised she was looking at a Daniel she had never seen before; a Daniel who did not seem to care that his feelings showed so plainly in his eyes, and in the the gentleness hovering about his usually firm, tight-lipped mouth.

'Oh, Daniel,' she whispered achingly, burying her face against him, and slipping her arms about his waist in order to press closer to him.

Her action seemed to act as a release, for he gathered her against him fiercely while at the same time his lips found hers with a hungry yearning as he kissed her again and again until the emotional storm within him subsided fractionally.

'Darling heart,' he whispered against her throat, his warm lips seeking a creamy, scented shoulder beneath the wide collar of her robe. 'Say the words I've been waiting so long to hear.'

'I love you, Daniel,' she whispered fervently, her arms locked about his neck. 'I loved you when I agreed to marry you, and, had I known that you loved me too, it wouldn't have been necessary to waste as much time as we have.'

'Don't remind me,' he laughed softly, a wicked gleam in his eyes as he raised his head slightly to look at her, taking in her flushed cheeks, the eyes sparkling with an inner glow, and the soft lips so unconsciously inviting his kisses. 'Lorelei, you have nothing on beneath this silky thing, I'm sure,' he murmured, his hands sliding down the length of her.

'Not a thing,' she admitted, her lips curved into a mischievous smile.

'Shameless hussy,' he reprimanded, his lips brushing against hers. 'Delightful little sea-nymph.' Her lips parted beneath his as his warm hands deliberately explored her body, awakening emotions that sharpened to a fierce desire before he held her away from him slightly. 'When will you be moving into that great big house up on the hill with me?'

'What about our divorce?' she asked, trying to think sanely.

'What divorce?' he grinned, indicating that her foolish request had been treated with disregard after all.

'What do I do with this flat, and the furniture?' she tried again, her heart beating so fast that she felt light-headed.

'Sell the furniture, and give up the lease of your flat, naturally.'

'By rights I should give a month's notice.'

Daniel's glance conveyed fierce disapproval. 'I'm an impatient man, my Lorelei, so pay them a double rental and be done with it.'

'What about my job in the theatre?'

'Matron and I have decided that you can stay on until a replacement can be found.' He frowned angrily. 'But I'm not waiting until then to make our marital status known.'

'But, Daniel——'

'No more quibbling,' he warned, the authority in his voice underlined by a sensual warmth. 'I want my wife where she belongs.'

'And where is that, may I ask?' she asked with mock innocence, glancing at him through lowered lashes, but her pulse quickened as his hands closed firmly about her waist and drew her closer.

'My wife's place is in my house, in my arms, and in my bed.'

'Daniel ... Daniel,' she sighed after a succession of kisses that left her weak and trembling in his arms. 'I love you so much.'

'Am I forgiven for treating you so badly that night you tried to tell me the truth?'

'Darling,' she kissed him on the side of his jaw. 'Didn't you know that love is eternal and it forgives anything and everything?'

'I thought of no one else but you during that year I spent in Switzerland,' he groaned, his arms tightening painfully about her. 'The way you smiled, the sound of your voice, and most of all the way you felt in my arms. So soft and warm, and so very desirable.' His lips found the frantic little pulse at the base of her throat and lingered. 'It drove me nearly mad at times when I thought that, had it not been for my idiotic behaviour, you could have been there with me instead of so many kilometres away, hating me, but never loving me.'

'Hush, my darling,' she whispered, running her fingers through his hair and loving the feel of its soft springiness.

'You never answered my question,' he reminded her. 'When are you moving in with me?'

'Tomorrow, if you want me to.'

His hands moved urgently against her back. 'And tonight?'

'I could always make up a bed for you on the sofa,' she offered mischievously, finding his outraged expression amusing.

'I can think of something far more comfortable than that, my love,' he said sternly, placing an arm behind her knees and lifting her as if she weighed nothing more than a child. 'From now on, Mrs Joanne Grant, your place is with your husband. Do I make myself clear?'

'Very clear, Dr Grant,' she smiled demurely, her arms tightening about his neck as she offered him her lips.

'Such obedience,' he murmured after a moment. 'It's marvellous what three little words can accomplish.'

'When they come from the heart they're not merely words, but a sacred vow,' she told him seriously, tracing a bold finger along the bridge of his nose before she followed the firm outline of his lips.

'Such wisdom, Lorelei, must be rewarded,' he told her, capturing her lips with his own as he carried her into her room where their soft laughter turned to urgent whispers, until two hearts beat as one in the stillness of that September night, with the promise of the future at last within their reach.

What readers say about Harlequin Romances

"Your books are the best I have ever found."
P.B.*, Bellevue, Washington

"I enjoy them more and more
with each passing year."
J.L., Spurlockville, West Virginia

"No matter how full and happy life might be,
it is an enchantment to sit
and read your novels."
D.K., Willowdale, Ontario

"I firmly believe that Harlequin Romances
are perfect for anyone who wants to read
a good romance."
C.R., Akron, Ohio

*Names available on request